트럭

도서출판 아시아에서는 《바이링궐 에디션 한국 대표 소설》을 기획하여 한국의 우수한 문학을 주제별로 엄선해 국내외 독자들에게 소개합니다. 이 기획은 국내외 우수한 번역가들이 참여하여 원작의 품격을 최대한 살렸습니다. 문학을 통해 아시아의 정체성과 가치를 살피는 데 주력해 온 도서출판 아시아는 한국인의 삶을 넓고 깊게 이해하는 데 이 기획이 기여하기를 기대합니다.

Asia Publishers presents some of the very best modern Korean literature to readers worldwide through its new Korean literature series 〈Bilingual Edition Modern Korean Literature〉. We are proud and happy to offer it in the most authoritative translation by renowned translators of Korean literature. We hope that this series helps to build solid bridges between citizens of the world and Koreans through a rich in-depth understanding of Korea.

바이링궐 에디션 한국 대표 소설 067
Bi-lingual Edition Modern Korean Literature 067

Truck

강영숙
트럭

Kang Young-sook

ASIA
PUBLISHERS

Contents

트럭

Truck

거친 황사 바람이 분다. 버려진 비닐봉지와 광고지들이 휙휙 허공으로 날아오른다. 남자는 하필이면 강남대로변의 패스트푸드점에서 만나자고 했다. 오랜만에 입은 치마가 고층 빌딩 사이로 몰아치는 돌풍에 맥없이 휘둘렸다. 햇볕은 따뜻했지만 눈도 제대로 뜰 수 없이 바람이 강해 먼지를 들쓴 구두만 내려다보고 걷는다. 성벽 위 요새처럼 회색 건물 하나가 눈앞에 버티고 서 있다. 바람 소리, 자동차 소리, 주변의 모든 장애물이 일순간 시야에서 사라지고 유독 그 5층 건물만이 환하게 부각된다. 다리 가랑이 속으로 말려들어간 치맛자락을 제대로 펴고 출입문을 밀고 들어간다.

Yellow dust bearing wind from China sweeps up from the street. Plastic bags and flyers soar up from the road and fly through the air. The man proposed to meet at a fast food restaurant on the main thoroughfare of Gangnam of all places. The skirt I'm wearing for the first time in a long while flutters helplessly, driven by gales of wind through the tall buildings. The sun is warm, but the wind is so fierce that I can't even open my eyes. I walk with my eyes fixed on my dust-covered shoes. A gray building comes up right before me, like a fortress. The sound of wind, the sound of cars. Suddenly, all obstacles disappear in front of my eyes. All I can

해서는 안 되는 일을 하는 사람들은 어떤 기미로든 서로를 알아본다. 인상착의나 이름 따위를 서로 말해두었다고는 해도 이름보다는 느낌으로 먼저 서로를 알아본다. 일렬로 놓인 의자에 앉아 뭔가 읽고 있는 마른 체구의 남자가 눈에 들어온다. 남자에게 다가가면서 다시 한 번 더 다짐을 한다. 절대로 우습게 보여서는 안 된다. 초보인 걸 들켜서 손해를 봐서는 안 된다.

이제 막 탄생 일주년이 되었다는 두툼한 불고기 햄버거의 생일을 기념하느라 매달아놓은 원색의 풍선들만 아니라면 밋밋할 만큼 단조로운 실내였다. 지나치게 커다랗게 들리는 음악 소리의 비트만큼이나 빠르게 심장이 뛰고, 나는 허둥대기 시작한다. 난 미스터 정입니다. 보고 있던 잡지를 접어 테이블 한쪽으로 밀어놓는 남자는 전화에서보다 톤이 낮은 목소리에 강단 있어 보이는 얼굴이다. 앉고 보니 남자와 거의 팔 한쪽이 붙을 지경이다. 최대한 남자와의 거리를 넓히려고 엉덩이를 빼지만 바닥에 고정시킨 의자이기에 도리가 없다. 이런 날은 일하기 싫죠? 남자는 자리를 불편해하는 기색을 읽었는지 잔뜩 세우고 있던 어깨에서 힘을 빼며 여유 있게 묻는다. 웬 바람이 이렇게 부는지요…… 남자는 허

see now is that bright building. After taking parts of my long skirt out from between my legs and smoothing them out; I push the door open and enter the restaurant.

Those who do things they shouldn't be doing can recognize each other somehow. They may have exchanged their names, features, and clothes before they meet, but they recognize each other not through their names but through the feelings they get from each other. A thin man reading something. I catch the man sitting on a chair from out of a line of chairs out of the corner of my eyes. I approach the man, and I talk to myself again under my breath. I shouldn't look like someone to be trifled with. I shouldn't look like a beginner and suffer any losses.

Save the colorful dangling balloons that celebrate the one-year anniversary of the thick *bulgogi* hamburger, the store looks somewhat bland. My heart beats as fast as the beat of blaring music, and I begin to feel flustered. *Mr. Jeong here*. The man folds the magazine he has been reading and pushes it aside. He has a lower-toned voice than what I remember hearing on the phone, and his face looks decisive and tenacious. I sit on the chair and realize

둥대는 모양이 신기한지 바람 어쩌구 하는 말에 슬며시 웃는다. 이런 일 언제부터 했어요, 처음이죠? 남자의 손가락에 걸린 반지가 햇빛에 빛난다. 뭔가 우습게 보이지 않기 위한 답변이 필요한 순간이다. 전에 다니던 회사에서 회원 자료 관리부에 있었어요. 아 그래요. 남자의 표정은 '너 이런 일 처음이지'에서 별로 달라지지 않는다. 갖고 있는 게 모두 몇 명이죠? 전부 육천이구요, 오늘은 일부만 갖고 나왔어요. 남자는 종이컵 테두리를 손가락으로 톡톡 치며 느릿느릿 움직이는 거리의 사람들에게 시선을 둔다.

사람들은 별스러울 것 없는 표정으로 패스트푸드점 안에서 길 쪽을 향해 나란히 앉아 있는 나와 남자에게는 관심을 두지 않는다. 그러나 나는 한번쯤 누군가 이 비밀 거래의 현장을 쳐다봐주었으면 했다. 만약 이 자리에서 남자와 헤어져 나가다 경찰에게 잡히게 된다면, 거리의 누군가는 남자와 나를 기억하게 될 것이 아닌가.

남자는 남은 커피를 다 마시고는 파삭 소리가 나도록 종이컵을 구겨버린다. 빨리 물건을 내놓으라는 표시처럼 느껴졌다. 인명 데이터베이스를 작성한 프로그램과

that my arm almost touches his. In order to lengthen the distance between us, I shift sideways, but it doesn't make too much difference because the chair is screwed onto the floor. *A day like this, who wants to work, huh?* Perhaps reading my discomfort from my gestures, he relaxes his shoulders and addresses me in an easy-going manner. *Goodness, what a wind!* The man grins at my complaint about the wind, probably finding my perturbed manner funny. *When did you start this line of work? This must be your first time, right?* A ring glints in his finger, refracted under the sunlight. I need to come up with an answer that will not make me look like someone to be trifled with. *I used to work at the data management office at my former workplace*, I say. *Oh, yeah?* His face doesn't change much from when he said, *This must be your first time, right?* He continues, *How many of them do you have?* I immediately respond with *Six thousand all together. I brought only a part of them today*. The man taps the rim of the paper cup in front of him, while leisurely watching people pass by outside.

People don't pay attention to this man and me facing the street with our ordinary facial expressions, sitting side by side inside a fast food restau-

주제어 설명 등이 담긴, 라벨이 붙은 디스켓 박스를 종이가방채로 남자에게 건네주었고, 남자는 곧바로 봉투를 내민다.

이렇게 해서 도둑질한 물건을 내다파는 내 생애 첫 번째 비밀 거래의 순간이 끝났다. 남자는 깃을 세운 코트를 입지도 않았고 색안경을 쓰지도 않았으며 우스꽝스러운 서류가방을 들고 있지도 않았다. 지하철 안에서 신문을 보다가 졸거나 휴대폰 벨소리에 놀라 들고 있던 신문을 떨어뜨리곤 하는, 누가 봐도 은밀한 거래 따위와는 거리가 멀어 보이는 평범한 인상이었다. 더구나 남자와 나를 감시하는 눈길은 어디에도 없지 않은가. 경천동지할 일이 일어날 줄만 알았던 거래는 너무나 싱거웠다. 그렇다고 비실비실 웃음이 비어져나오지도 않았다. 남자의 뒷모습은 보이지 않았다. 그저 피로한 나머지 집으로 가는 길이 멀게만 느껴졌다.

축축한 방바닥에 전신을 대고 누워, 떠올랐다 사라지고 다시 떠오르는 내다 판 이름들의 환영에 쫓긴다. 현미경으로 들여다본 미생물의 백색 꿈틀거림처럼 하나하나의 이름들이 흐린 형광등 아래에서 거대한 덩어리로 뭉쳐졌다가는 흩어지고 다시 뭉쳐져 내 온몸을 짓누

rant. I wish someone saw our secret transaction. If we get arrested on our separate ways out of this restaurant, at least then someone on the street would remember us!

The man finishes his coffee and crumples his paper cup loudly. It sounds as if he is telling me to show him the stuff quickly. I hand him the paper bag with the labeled diskette box full of programs used for creating the database and guides explaining keywords. The man immediately hands me an envelope.

This was how my first secret transaction for stolen goods ended. The man wasn't wearing a coat with his collar turned up. He wasn't wearing sunglasses or carrying a ridiculous-looking briefcase, either. He looked like someone who would doze off reading a newspaper or drop his newspaper on a subway train at the sound of his ringtone. An average man who looked as far as possible from someone who would conduct a secret transaction. Additionally, there was no surveillance on us! The transaction that seemed as if it would create a sensation across the whole world was so ordinary. That didn't make me unable to suppress involuntary smile, though. I couldn't see the man any

른다. 어두운 고속도로 위를 달리는 자동차 소리까지도 망각될 만큼, 온몸을 짓누르는 압력이 결코 만만치 않다.

운전면허학원 강사들의 노란 자동차가 왔다. 운전면허학원은 집들보다 좀 높은 산 중턱에 있다. 야간 도로주행 강습을 끝내고 운전면허학원으로 들어가기 전, 그들은 집에서 좀 떨어진 이면도로 한켠에 차를 세우고 키들키들 웃으면서 담배를 피운다. 오물을 실은 청소차들이 줄지어 하치장으로 들어가는 시간도 바로 이 저녁시간이다. 청소차는 차량 통행이 뜸한 한밤중이나 새벽에만 운행한다. 그리고 숨죽이며 잔뜩 웅크리고 있는 몇 채 안 되는 집들.

아버지는 동그랗게 몸을 말고 텔레비전 쪽으로 시선을 두고 있다. 텔레비전은 국적도 알 수 없는 노화방지 화장품 광고를 하고 있다. 발라도 발라도 주름이 펴지지 않을 것처럼 보이는 얼굴의 나이 많은 서양 여자는 화장품 선전을 위해 애써 웃는다. 탁월한 효과를 보았다고 흥분하는 여자의 얼굴이 외롭게 흔들린다.

거실 창문을 연다. 창밖은 짙은 회색이지만 고속도로 위의 하늘은 딴 세상처럼 새파랗다. 뿌옇게 낮은 하늘

more. I was just so tired that my way home felt very far.

Sprawling on the floor, I am chased by visions of the names I sold. They keep appearing and disappearing. Like white microbes wriggling under the microscope, the names gather to form an enormous mass, scatter, and then lump together under the dimly lit florescent light to weigh my entire body down. The pressure from the mass over my entire body is quite substantial, so much so that I can even forget the car noise from the darkened highway outside.

The yellow cars the teachers at the driving school use approach. The driving school is located on the mid-slope of the hill, a little higher than all the neighborhood houses. Before they go back to the driving school, the teachers park their cars on a side of the narrow road and smoke, giggling amongst themselves. This is also when the garbage trucks go back to the depository one after another, forming a line as they go. Garbage trucks come and go only in the middle of the night or very early in the morning, when there's less traffic. Then, below the depository, a few houses huddle quietly.

Father is crouching and watching TV. An adver-

저 끝까지 올려다보면 물방울처럼 반짝거리는 별들이 보인다. 이곳으로 처음 이사 왔을 때만 해도 파란 하늘, 빛나는 별 따위는 눈에 들어오지 않았다. 고속도로를 질주하는 자동차 소리, 쓰레기 하치장에서 들려오는 반복적인 기계음은 아버지와 나를 늘 방 안에만 있게 했다. 창밖을 내다보고 있으면 마음은 이미 터덕터덕 길 위로 나가 있지만 아직까지 나는 밤 산책을 하지 못한다.

거실 쪽 베란다 너머로 고속도로가 보인다. 고속도로를 비추는 불빛의 세기가 점차 흐려진다. 라디오를 낮게 틀어두는 것도 시간을 보내는 데는 도움이 된다. 바람에 흩날리는 불씨처럼 점점이 사라지는 자동차들을 보고 있으면 시간이 갈수록 점점 더 뚜렷해지는 하나의 그림 속으로 빠져들게 된다.

얼굴에 기미가 잔뜩 오른, 왠지 바싹바싹 침이 마르는 느낌을 주는 여자가 연못가의 낮은 집 창 앞에 앉아 있다. 처음에는 여자 하나가 창 앞에 앉아 있는 데서 시작된 이 그림은 여자가 창틀에 턱을 괴고 앉아 어딘가를 바라보고 있는 모습으로 옮겨간다. 여자의 머리 위로 수십 마리의 날파리가 날지만 여자는 자세를 흩뜨리거나 창문 앞을 떠나지 않는다. 또 여자는 해가 쨍쨍한 대

tisement for some anti-aging cosmetics is on. A very old Western woman, her face wrinkled so much it looks as if her skin will never become smooth again, squeezes out a smile for the cosmetics advertisement. The woman's face, enthusiastically testifying to the outstanding effects of the product, is lonely and trembles.

I open the living room window. It's dark gray outside the window, but the sky over the highway is bright blue as if it belongs to another world. I look up and scan the entire expanse of the hazy, low hung sky. In the sky there are shimmering stars like dewdrops. When Father and I first moved here, I could see neither the blue sky nor the stars. The noise from the cars speeding on the highway and the constant droning mechanical noise coming from the garbage depository imprisoned Father and me to our rooms. When I look out the window, my heart is already out and trudging down the road. But I haven't tried a night stroll yet.

I can see the highway over the veranda in front of the living room. The light over the highway gets weaker. Leaving your radio on at a low volume helps you pass the time. If you watch cars disappear one by one like sparks blown out by the

낮에 솜털이 까실까실한 살구를 소쿠리째 끌어안고 베어먹거나 옥수수기름에 바싹 튀긴 미꾸라지를 한 움큼씩 입에 털어넣고 와삭와삭 소리를 내며 씹어 먹는다. 꿈속에서인지, 아니면 그 옛날 어디에서인지 나는 그런 여자를 본 적이 있다. 여자가 혹시 과거의 나는 아닐까, 아니, 어쩌면 그것은 언젠가 본 이국 풍경의 사진에 덧칠된 환영일지도 모른다. 여자는 낮에는 창 앞을 지키다 밤에만 나와 연못으로 들어가 몸을 담근다. 연못은 중심부만 물이 돌고 자갈과 진흙이 깔린 바닥은 바짝 말라붙어 있다. 연못 근처에 살았던 적이 있었는지 불행하게도 내게는 기억이 없다.

벌써 덥구나. 창문이라도 열지 그러냐.

마루로 나오시지 왜 방에만 계세요. 아버지도 알잖아요. 꽃가루 때문에 창문을 열어둘 수가 없다는 걸.

아버지는 내의만 입은 채로 텔레비전 화면을 쳐다보고 있다. 저희들끼리 경중경중 뛰면서 깔깔대는 휴일 저녁의 텔레비전 프로그램은 누구나 삼십 분만 보면 싫증을 내거나 소외감을 느낄 만하건만, 아버지는 언제나 고요히 그들만의 유희를 지켜본다.

아버지 물 좀 드려요?

wind, you find yourself immersed in a picture that becomes clearer as time passes.

A woman with a heavily freckled face, who somehow gives you the impression that her mouth is drying up, is sitting in front of a window of a low house near the pond. This picture that began with a woman sitting in front of a window changes into one where a woman is watching somewhere with her chin resting on the hands. Although dozens of flies buzz around her head, she neither changes her posture nor leaves the window. The woman sometimes takes fluffy apricots directly out of the basket under the noonday sun and bites them, or chews a handful of corn oil deep-fried mudfishes with her mouth closed and with a loud rustling sound. I'm not sure if it was in a dream or if it was sometime in the past, but I have seen this woman somewhere. Could she be myself from the past, perhaps? No, maybe, it's just a modified vision of an exotic photograph I've seen some time ago. The woman stays put in front of the window only during the day. It is only at night that she comes out of her house and dips her body into the pond. There's water in the middle of the pond. Along the periphery, the gravel and mud floor is dried up com-

됐다.

그럼 정종이라도 한잔 데워드려요?

됐다.

아버지의 등에 스웨터를 걸쳐준다. 아버지의 등 골격은 점점 더 참담하게 드러난다. 텔레비전 전파에 둘러싸인 아버지의 마른 몸은 무게감 없이 기괴하게 보인다. 나는 아버지가 무슨 생각을 하는지 잘 모른다. 늘 함께 있는 사람일수록 머릿속을 잘 알기는 쉽지 않은 것 같다.

작년 늦봄이었을 것이다. 아버지가 아주 늦게 귀가한 날이 있었다. 아버지의 얼굴은 핏기 없이 노랗게 들떠 있었고, 밥을 차려줘도 먹지를 않았다. 아버지는 세수도 하지 않고 곧바로 자리에 누웠다. 그뿐이었다. 그런데 문단속을 하러 현관으로 나가보니 아버지의 신발이 이상했다. 신발 안에 흰 꽃잎들이 그득했다. 뭉그러졌지만 금세 그 꽃 이름을 알 수 있었다. 아버지가 들어오고부터 줄곧 코끝을 따라다닌 것은 아까시나무 꽃냄새였다. 방으로 들어가 아버지가 벗어 걸어둔 옷을 살폈다. 꽃잎은 중절모 한켠에도 묻어 있었고, 양복 겉주머니, 그리고 안경집 틈새까지도 드문드문 묻어 있었다.

pletely. Unfortunately, I don't have a memory of having lived near a pond.

"It's hot already. Why don't you open the window?"

"Why don't you come out of your room and stay in the living room? You know, Father, that we can't leave the windows open because of the pollen, don't you?"

Father is staring at TV, wearing only undershirt and underpants. Anybody would feel bored or alienated after watching that weekend evening TV program for thirty minutes, a program where people just frolic and giggle amongst themselves, but Father always watches this game show without saying a word.

"Would you like some water, Father?"

"That's okay."

"Would you like a bowl of warm *jeongjong*, then?"

"That's okay."

I cover his back with a sweater. The bones along his back are becoming even more pitiably visible. Bathed in the light waves of the TV, his fragile, weightless body looks grotesque. I don't know very well what Father thinks. It seems harder for you to know what's in the mind of someone you always

꽃잎과 한바탕 씨름이라도 하고 들어온 것 같았다. 그날 이후 꽃잎을 묻혀 들어오는 일은 없었지만 계절이 바뀔수록 아버지는 점점 더 고요해졌다. 우연하게도 그 일이 있은 지 며칠 후 아버지와 나는 이 집을 발견했고, 방 두 개에서 살았다던 여섯 식구들은 이삿짐 차를 먼저 떠나보내고 이면도로를 따라 줄지어 걸어서 이사를 갔다.

시간이 얼마나 지났을까. 아버지는 또 텔레비전을 켜놓은 채 잠이 들고, 나는 아버지의 마른 몸에 이불을 덮어주고 물 한 그릇을 떠다 머리맡에 놓아준다. 비좁고 낡은 집을 비추는 불을 차례로 끄고 내 방으로 들어가 눕는다. 줄곧 불안감에 시달려서인지 시간이 갈수록 정신은 점점 더 또렷해지고 잠도 오지 않는다. 아버지의 방에 다시 들어간다. 아버지의 숨소리를 확인한다. 고요한 밤이면 가끔씩 아버지의 숨소리를 확인하곤 한다. 죽은 사람처럼 움직임이 없는 아버지의 몸은 아주 더디게, 조금씩 숨을 쉰다.

어느새 새벽이다. 어디선가 휘파람 소리가 섞인 노랫소리가 간간이 들린다. 새벽녘에 한 번도 들어보지 못한 소리가 가까운 데서부터 들려온다. 무거운 것을 땅

live with.

It happened late spring last year. Father came home very late that night. His face looked pale, yellowish, and worn, and he refused to eat the dinner I'd prepared for him. He didn't wash his face and went straight to his bed. That was all. When I went to the hallway to lock the door, his shoes looked a little strange. They were full of flower petals. Although the petals were crushed, I could immediately tell what they were. I had smelled the black locust flowers since he had come home. I went into his room and checked his clothes and hat. There were petals all over his clothes—on the side of his hat, the outside pocket of his jacket, and even in the seams of his eyeglass case. It looked as if he had come home after a wrestling match with a bed of flower petals. Since that day, he never came home with clothes full of petals, but as the seasons came and went, he became gradually quieter. Incidentally, a few days after that night Father and I found this house. The family of six who had lived in this two-bedroom house walked along the narrow road in a line after sending their stuff on a moving company truck.

How long had it been? Father fell asleep again,

위에 부리는 듯한 소리도 들린다. 나는 무슨 생각에서인지 그 소리에 이끌려 입고 있는 채로 문을 열고 밖으로 나간다. 아직 어둠이 살아 있는 새벽이다.

저 아래 일방통행로에서부터 청소차가 천천히 집 앞을 지나 하치장 쪽으로 달리고 있다. 청소원 두 사람이 양쪽에 매달려 있다. 새벽의 청소차를 슬리퍼를 신은 한 남자가 뛰어서 따라오고 있다. 남자의 얼굴은 환하게 웃고 있는데, 청소원들은 늘 그렇다는 듯이 막무가내로 뛰어오는 남자는 쳐다보지도 않는다. 도무지 나이를 알 수 없는 남자다. 새벽녘에 청소차를 좇아 뛰어가는 남자의 집은 어디일까. 청소차가 남자를 따돌리듯 빠르게 회전해 하치장 쪽으로 올라가고 뒤따라가던 슬리퍼의 남자는 아우성을 치며 하치장 쪽으로 뛰어간다. 그가 왜 청소차를 따라가는지는 그만이 알 것이다.

집에서 좀 떨어진 도로변에 커다란 트럭이 서 있다. 반소매 차림의 남자가 운전석에서 조수석으로, 다시 짐을 실은 트럭 뒤쪽으로 분주히 오가고 있다. 남자는 키가 크고 몸집이 아주 크다. 남자는 고무 발깔개를 꺼내 플라타너스 기둥에 탁탁 턴 뒤 다시 운전석에 깐다. 가래침도 뱉고 헛기침도 하고, 트럭은 장거리 경주를 준

the TV still on. I cover his wasted body with a blanket, get a glass of water, and leave it by his bed. I turn off lights in this cramped old house one after another, go to my room, and lie down. Perhaps, because I've been anxious all day, I can't fall asleep; I feel even more awake as time passes by. I go to Father's room again. I check his breathing. On quiet nights I sometimes check his breathing. Father's body, immovable as a corpse, inhales and exhales after long intervals and only very slightly.

It's dawn already. The sound of singing mixed with whistling reaches me occasionally from somewhere. An unusual sound I haven't heard around that time comes from somewhere nearby. I can hear something heavy being unloaded on the road. I am drawn to that sound for some reason, and I open the door and leave the house without changing my clothes. It's still somewhat dark outside. It's still dawn.

A garbage truck passes by our house slowly from the one-way street below my house and in the direction of the depository. Two garbage workers hang from both sides of the truck. A man wearing slippers runs after the truck. He is smiling brightly. The garbage workers do not even look at him, as if

비하는 것처럼 분주하다. 사면이 막힌 커다란 컨테이너 박스 짐칸을 등에 얹은 트럭은 앞바퀴만 해도 네 개나 된다. 트럭 너머로 말갛게 하늘이 보인다. 아침 햇살에 트럭의 몸체가 환하게 빛난다.

지난번엔 큰 도움이 됐습니다. 한 번 더 만날 수 있을까요.

전화 속 남자의 목소리는 여전히 불쾌한 느낌을 준다.

왜 만나자고 하시는지.

남자와 전화를 끊고 나서부터 또다시 가슴이 뛴다. 다시 연락이 왔다는 건 넘긴 명단이 쓸모가 있었다는 뜻임이 분명했다. 나는 바보가 아니지 않은가.

남자에게 건네준 명단은 전에 다니던 회사에서 가장 낮은 단계의 등급을 매겨 분류한 일반 회원들이었다. 나는 육천 명 정도의 회원을 관리하는 관리부에 소속되어 있었는데 그중 이천 명 정도에 대해서는 주소나 이름 전화번호 등의 기본 정보밖에 없었다. 그렇다고 흑백 프린터로 인쇄되어 나와 길거리 붕어빵 장수가 사용할 만큼 값싼 정보는 아니었다. 어쨌든 나머지 사천, 그중에서도 이천에 대한 자료는 주민등록번호와 가족 사

nothing at all is extraordinary about his actions. I cannot guess the man's age. Where does he live, this man running after a garbage truck at dawn? The garbage truck turns around the corner and rumbles up towards the depository as if to shake him off, and the man runs after it, leaping and yelling. Only he must know why he is following after a garbage truck.

A large truck is parked on the side of the road a little ways away from my house. A man in short sleeves hurries about, from the driver's seat to the passenger seat, and then to the back of the truck. The man is tall and heavy. He removes a floor mat from the driver's seat of the truck, dusts it against the side of sycamore trunk, and then puts it back. He spits and clears his throat. He looks busy, as if he's preparing for long-distance travel. The truck carries an enormous sealed trailer and has four front wheels. I can see the clear sky beyond the truck. The body of the truck gleams under the morning sun.

"It was a great help last time. May I see you again?"

I still find the man's voice unpleasant on the

항, 신용카드번호는 물론 자주 이용하는 쇼핑센터와 기호품 목록까지도 죄다 알 수 있는 고급 정보였다.

나는 일을 그르치고 싶지는 않았다. 몇 년 전에 입었던 정장을 꺼내 다림질을 했다. 살이 오른 탓에 어깨가 끼어 불편했지만 남자에게 사무적인 느낌을 주고 싶었다. 은근히 무시하는 듯한 그 표정과 말투 때문에라도 좀 끼는 옷을 입는 고통쯤은 참아야 할 것 같았다. 남자는 종로의 한 레스토랑을 두 번째 비밀 거래 장소로 택했다.

지난번엔 차 대접도 못 해서 죄송했습니다. 뭘 시키죠? 난 밥을 좀 먹어야겠는데……

남자는 예의로라도 내게 밥을 먹겠느냐고 물어야 하는데, 내 의사 따위는 묻지도 않고 자기가 먹을 김치볶음밥만 시킨다. 남자가 밥을 먹는 동안 이동통신회사에서 설치한 가판대 앞에서 요란한 몸짓으로 움직이고 있는 내레이터 모델들을 쳐다본다. 남자는 수저질 몇 번으로 식사를 끝내고는 후식으로 나오는 커피를 마신다. 나는 소갈증이 난 사람처럼 계속해서 냉수를 들이켠다. 물잔을 뚫어져라 내려다보며, 다짐 또 다짐을 한다. 이번에는 전보다 더 많은 돈을 받아야만 한다.

phone.

"What can I do for you?"

I hang up and I feel excited again. He called me, so it clearly must mean that my list was useful. I'm no fool, am I?

The list I handed the man last time was a list of general members of the company I used to work for, members who belonged to the lowest membership level. I worked in the membership department, which managed about six thousand members. For two thousand of the members, there was only basic information, like their names, addresses, and phone numbers. Still, the information was worth more than just to make the black-and-white printouts into wrapping papers for the fish-shaped waffles sold on the streets. At any rate, the information for the remaining four thousand members, especially for a particular two thousand of them, was at a high-class level because it included not only member resident registration numbers, family information, and credit card numbers, but also the shopping centers they frequently used and the list of merchandise items they liked.

I don't want to ruin this work. I take out and iron a suit I used to wear a few years ago. I'm a little

이번엔 금액을 좀 올려주셨으면 좋겠어요.

그래요? 그럼 우선 오늘은 전과 같이 드리고, 상세한 평가를 한 후에 더 드리죠.

그럼 전 팔지 않겠어요. 이번에 더 주시지 않으면 다른 쪽으로 팔 생각이에요. 거래할 곳도 물색했고……

남자는 내 말을 자르듯 봉투를 내밀며, 입술 한쪽을 지그시 누른다.

벌어먹여야 할 아이들이 있어 보이지도 않는데 지독하군! 며칠 내로 곧 연락을 하죠. 내가 거래하는 쪽에도 시간을 줘야 하니까.

그래도 안 되겠어요. 벌어먹여야 할 노인이 계세요. 꽃구경을 보내드려야 해요.

오금을 펴지 못할 만큼 긴장해서 또박또박 말했건만 남자는 꽃구경이라는 말 때문인지 어이없다는 듯 피식 웃는다. 그리고 지갑에서 만 원짜리 몇 장을 더 꺼내 내민 봉투 위에 포개놓는다. 그리고 잠시 침묵. 남자는 절대 다시 만나고 싶지 않은 사람이었다. 남자가 일어나 먼저 레스토랑을 나갔고 나는 무조건 그와 반대 방향으로 걷기 시작했다. 화가 났다.

남자는 아주 어렵게 만났다. 남자를 만나기까지 여섯

uncomfortable because the suit is too tight, especially around the shoulders because I've gotten bigger. But I want to give the man a more business-like impression than before. I feel like I should be able to stand the kind of discomfort that comes from wearing a tight suit, considering his facial expression and speech manner that seemed to suggest his disregard for me the last time. The man suggested a restaurant in Jongno as the location for our second secret transaction.

"I'm sorry that I didn't even treat you with tea last time. What shall I order? I'd like to have some rice..."

The man orders kimchi fried rice for himself, without even pretending to be polite and asking me what I want. While he eats his food, I look at the spokesmen making large, dramatic gestures in front of the mobile communications company stand. The man finishes eating after a few spoonfuls and then drinks the coffee that accompanies the meal. I keep drinking cold water like someone suffering from a constant thirst. I stare at the glass and tell myself over and over again that I should get more than what I got last time.

"I'd like to be paid more this time."

사람을 거쳐야 했다. 고등학교 동창 중에서 백화점을 다니는 남자와 결혼했다는, 이름도 잘 기억나지 않는 친구에게 무조건 전화를 걸었다. 그 남편은 다른 한 남자를 소개했다. 그 남자는 광고 사정상 업체를 밝힐 수 없다는 브랜드의 양복을 빼곡이 걸고 저가 할인매장을 열고 있었다. 그 매장에 걸려 있던 옷들은 하나같이 상표가 찢겨나간 채였다. 그 남자는 휴대폰 고리를 질근질근 씹으며 제 애인 얘기만 하던 통신판매회사 여직원을 소개했다. 여자는 그 자리에서 변두리 쇼핑센터의 영업 담당 직원과, 지금은 직장에 다니지 않지만 제법 큰 카드회사에 다녔다는 주부를 소개했는데, 카드회사에 다녔다는 여자는 나를 노래방으로 끌고 가 두 시간 동안 줄기차게 혼자서 노래를 불렀다.

그리고 한동안 아무도 연락이 없었다. 그러다가 전화가 왔다. 누가 누구를 소개했고, 누구한테 소개받아 당신을 알게 되었다고 얘기하는 과정이 그들 사이에서는 불필요했는지, 전화를 걸어온 남자는 내가 한 번도 만난 적이 없는 모르는 사람의 이름을 댔다. 그들이 모두 한통속이 되어 나란히 서서 이 거래의 전모를 밝히겠다고 나서는 것은 아닌지, 나는 이번 만남이 왠지 불안했

"Oh yes? Well, I'll pay you the same today, and then I'll give you more after I take a close look at the information you've given me today."

"I can't sell it to you then. I'm planning to sell it to someone else, if you're not willing to pay me more. I have other buyers..."

The man pushes an envelope towards me, as if to cut me off, and bites the side of his lip.

"I have children to feed. I can't check the information now so this is outrageous! I'll contact you in a few days. I have to give my buyer some time, too, you know."

"No matter. I have a senior to feed as well. I have to send him to a flower-viewing."

Although I say this syllable by syllable, my voice tight with nerves, the man grins, as if to tell me that this is all bullshit, perhaps because of the "flower-viewing" I mentioned. Then, he opens his wallet, takes out a few ten thousand *won* notes and places them on top of the envelope. A few seconds of silence. He is the kind of man I never want to meet again. He stands up first and leaves the restaurant. I get up a few moments later and begin to walk in the opposite direction without even thinking about it. I am angry.

다. 내 생애 두 번째 비밀 거래는 이렇게 불쾌하고 엉성하게 끝이 났다.

트럭은 밤에만 움직인다. 엊그제는 자극적인 휘발성 염료 냄새를 피우더니, 오늘은 썩은 생선 냄새를 풍기며 시동을 건 채 서 있다. 남자의 얼굴은 잘 보이지 않지만 불이 켜진 트럭 안에서 남자는 휴대폰을 들고 전화를 걸기도 하고 뭔가를 먹기도 한다. 나는 남자의 실루엣이 집 쪽으로 움직일 때마다 남자가 나를 쳐다보고 있는 것 같아 커튼을 친다. 그러나 금세 다시 커튼을 여는 건 오히려 내 쪽이다.

양치질을 하고 세수를 하는 동안 트럭의 휘파람 소리가 달게 들린다. 남자는 트럭 옆자리에 누군가 한 사람 앉기만 하면 길을 떠날지도 모른다. 바르지 않던 화장수를 바르는 내 얼굴을 비춘 거울은 깨진 거울이 아니라 황금 거울이다. 감이 얇고 폭이 넓은 꽃무늬 치마를 입고, 발길에 닿는 돌부리는 경쾌하게 걷어차며 걷는다. 어느새 튼튼한 고무 타이어를 단 트럭이 당당하게 내 눈앞에 서 있다.

남자는 드라이버를 들고 러닝셔츠를 입은 채 트럭 한 귀퉁이의 나사를 조이고 있다. 남자는 라이트를 켜놓고

I met this man after so much trouble. I had to go through so many people in order to meet him. I called a high school alumna, who was known to have married a man working at a department store. I couldn't even remember her name very easily. Her husband connected me with another man. He was an owner of a discount suit store, which was full of suits whose brands could never be made public because of brand image concerns, according to him. All the clothes hanging in that store had the brand name tags cut off of them. This man introduced me to a woman working at a mail-order firm. This woman almost only talked about her boyfriend the entire time, chewing the handle of her cellphone as she went on and on. She then introduced me to a clerk in charge of business operations at a shopping center on the outskirts of a city and a housewife who was supposed to have worked at a large credit card company, although she no longer did now. This supposed former credit card company employee dragged me to a *karaoke* room and sang for two hours by herself.

Then, there was no news for a while until I got a phone call one day. Perhaps, it was unnecessary for him to explain who introduced who when he

작업을 한다. 어둠 속에서도 트럭의 외장은 화려한 은색이다. 나는 작업 중인 그의 등 뒤에 말없이 서 있었고, 그는 등을 돌려 나를 보자마자 손에 들고 있던 드라이버를 내던지고 운전석으로 올라앉아 내게 손을 내밀었다. 믿을 수 없는 일이 일어난 것이다. 그의 손은 패스트푸드점에서 봤던 버릇없는 그 남자의 손의 두 배쯤 되는 크기였고 미세한 밀가루 조직을 덮어씌운 듯 부드러워 보였다. 웬만한 사람은 한 방에 날릴 수도 있을 만큼 큰 손이었다. 남자는 그 큰 손을 청바지 위 허벅지에 올려놓았는데 자꾸만 그 손을 만져보고 싶은 충동이 일었다. 남자 옆자리에 앉아 넘겨다본 우리 집은 아주 작은 상자 같았고, 조금씩 새어나오는 불빛은 개똥벌레 불빛만큼이나 약했다.

트럭이 처음 온 그날부터 보고 있었어요.

난 하도 돌아다녀서 언제 여길 왔는지 몰라요.

남자의 얼굴은 땀으로 번들거렸다. 남자는 내가 손가락을 꼽아가며 트럭이 온 날을 세는 동안 생수통을 입에 대고 벌컥벌컥 물을 들이마셨다.

파란 싹들만 있었는데 어느새 꽃이라니.

갑자기 생기가 넘치는 내 목소리가 왠지 어색했다. 남

got to me. The man on the phone just gave me the name of a person I'd never met before.

I feel uncomfortable about this second meeting, worried that for some reason they might all stand before me in a line and come forward to reveal the entire processes of the deal. The second secret transaction in my life left a bad taste in my mouth. I feel disconcerted and unsettled.

The truck only moves around at night. A few days ago it reeked of volatile dyes. Today, with its engine already started, it smells like rotten fish. Although I can't see the man's face well, he sometimes talks on his cellphone and other times eats something under the truck's inner light. Whenever his silhouette turns in the direction of my house, I am afraid that he might be watching me, and I draw the curtains. Still, it's me who sweeps the curtains open again.

As I brush my teeth and wash my face, I hear a merry whistling sound coming from the truck. The man might start his trip as soon as someone comes to take a seat next to him. The mirror that I put on face lotion in front of, which I wouldn't normally do, is not broken, but golden. I decide to put a flower-patterned skirt made of a thin wide fabric,

자는 생각났다는 듯이 휘 주변을 둘러봤다.

그런데, 저 뒤에 뭐가 있는지 물어봐도 돼요?

짐칸을 가리키는 손짓에 남자는 싱겁다는 듯이 웃기만 했다. 트럭 안에는 모든 게 다 있었다. 수많은 장난감이 있는 방에 처음 들어간 아이처럼 정신없이 트럭 안을 살펴봤다. 카키색 담요와 두툼한 솜이불, 뜯지 않은 생수병들과 컵라면이 가득 든 상자, 휴대용 가스레인지와 일회용 종이컵들, 카드와 화투 몇 갑, 헤어 무스와 칫솔 치약, 소형 카메라와 지도책, 성경책과 만화책까지. 게다가 큰 가슴을 내놓고 있는 여자의 사진이 실린 잡지와 날짜 지난 신문까지 트럭 안에는 없는 것이 없었다.

남자는 내가 트럭 안을 살펴보는 사이 실내등을 포함한 트럭의 모든 불을 환하게 켰다. 그리고 라디오 볼륨을 올렸다. 봄밤의 트럭 불빛에 출렁이는 꽃가루들의 춤을 본 적이 있는가. 남자에게서 나는 쿰쿰한 땀냄새와 트럭 엔진에서 풍기는 기름 냄새, 그리고 꽃가루. 식물성과 광물성의 우연한 어울림에 나도 모르게 탄성이 흘러나왔다. 내가 흥분하면 할수록 꽃가루들은 더욱더 자유롭게 떠다녔다.

트럭은 서 있는 것이 분명했지만 세상의 그 어딜 가

and I step out from my doorway and begin to make my way over to the truck, randomly kicking whatever rocks along the way. Suddenly, a truck with solid rubber tires looms before me.

The man wears an undershirt and is screwing in a bolt into the corner of the truck. He is working with the truck light on. In the dark, the truck is splendid silver. I stand behind him silently as he works. He turns around and, as soon as he sees me, he tosses away his screwdriver, gets into the driver's seat, and sticks his hand out towards me. Something unbelievable has happened. His hand is about twice as big as that of the rude man I met at the fast food restaurant. It looks soft, as if it was covered in fine flour. His hand is so large that it looks as if he could send an ordinary man flying in one blow. The man places that giant hand over his denim-clad thigh. I feel an irresistible impulse to touch that hand. Sitting next to him, my house looks like a tiny box and the light seeping out of it looks as weak as a firefly's.

"I've been watching you since your truck first arrived here."

"I've been traveling around so much that I can't remember when I first came here."

도 괜찮을 고무 타이어로 쭉 뻗은 길을 향해 달리고 있는 것만 같았다. 등받이에 머리를 대고 기대어 앉은 남자 가슴 가까이 다가갔다. 내 머리가 정확히 남자의 가슴께에 닿았다. 땀에 전 그의 셔츠에서 생선 냄새가 났지만 그의 가슴에 머리를 기댔다. 그리고 그에게 물었다. 이 차는 언제 달리죠? 그가 대답했다. 혹시 도, 돈이 필요한가요? 그의 가슴이 쾅쾅 울렸다.

고등학교를 졸업하고 사무 보조원으로 시작해서 꼭 십 년을 다닌 회사였다. 말 그대로 사무 보조 업무는 무척이나 단순해서, 그 누구라도 몇 시간 설명만 들으면 할 수 있는 일이었다. 그러나 그렇게 쉬운 일도 오래 지속되자 옥석을 가릴 줄 아는 눈을 만들어주었다.

파일들을 빼내오던 날은 토요일이었다. 그 전날인 금요일 저녁에 송별회를 했고, 간단한 짐 정리만 토요일 오후에 할 생각이었다. 사무실에는 토요일 근무인 직원들만 점심을 먹은 후 의자에 기대어 자고 있었다. 아무도 내가 뭘 하는지 와서 들여다보는 사람이 없었다. 책상 속에서 칫솔이며 손거울, 의료보험카드와 월급명세서 따위를 챙겨 가방 속에 넣었다. 그리고 습관처럼 늘

The man's face glistens with sweat. As I count out the days when the truck first arrived with my fingers, the man gulps down water from a bottle of distilled water.

"The plants were just beginning to bud then. And now there are flowers. Time flies!"

My suddenly lively voice sounds awkward. The man suddenly looks around as if remembering something.

"By the way, may I ask you what's in the back?" I ask.

When I point to the back of the truck, the man simply grins as if to say that's a pointless question. There are all kinds of things in the truck. I look around all over inside the truck like a child entering a room full of toys for the first time. A khaki blanket, a thick cotton comforter, a box full of unopened distilled water bottles and instant cup noodles, a gas burner stove and paper cups, playing cards and a few packs of *hwatu* cards, a can of hair mousse, a toothbrush and some toothpaste, a small camera and maps and a bible and some comic books. Additionally, there's an old newspaper and a magazine with a photo of a large-breasted topless woman. There's everything inside this truck.

사용하던 컴퓨터를 작동시켰다. 일을 할 때는 너무나 중요해서 비밀번호 목록까지 만들어 관리하던 파일들이었으나 정리하는 마당에 읽어보니 보관할 가치도 없어 보이는 것들이 수두룩했다. 그런 파일들을 지웠다. 그리고 늘 전화로, 회신엽서로, 통신으로 관리했던 회원 정보 파일을 열었고, 순간 섭섭함을 느꼈다. 십 년을 일했다는 증거로 그냥 가지고 있고 싶었다. 졸고 있던 직원에게 인사를 하고 사무실을 나와서 여직원들과 자주 갔던 분식집으로 갔다. 삶은 계란을 포크로 부숴 넣어가며 아주 매운 떡볶이를 먹었다. 다 먹고 분식집을 나오는데 종업원이 불렀다. 얼굴을 알아보고 인사라도 하려나 했지만 내 가슴에 그려진 붉은 고춧가루 흔적을 알려주기 위해서였다.

남자가 전화를 걸어왔다. 내가 갖고 있다는 그 마지막 이천 명의 명단을 사고 싶다고 했다. 나는 지난번 거래 이후로, 남자가 전화를 해올 거라고는 생각하지 않았다. 나는 마지막 거래를 좀더 확실하게 하고 싶었다. 저녁이었다. 남자가 지정한 장소인 장충단공원으로 나갔다. 한 번도 가본 적이 없는 곳이었다. 공원 안의 테니스장에서 간간이 공 치는 소리가 들려올 뿐 한산한 곳이

While I look around inside the truck, the man turns on all the truck's lights including its inner light. Then, he turns the radio volume on high. Have you ever seen pollen dance in shafts of a truck's lights? The sour sweat smell from a man and the smell of gasoline from a truck engine, and pollen. The sudden union of plant and mineral makes me groan without intending to. The more excited I become, the freer the pollens float.

Although the truck is clearly standing still, it feels as if it is gliding along a straight road on those solid rubber tires. I move in close to the man as he leans into the back of his seat. My head touches the exact center of his chest. Although I can smell fish from his sweat-soaked shirt, I lean into him. And I ask, *When does this truck run?* He stutters, *Do you by any chance need m-money?* His heart is pounding.

I worked at the company for ten years since I started working as its attendant immediately after graduating from high school. The work I did as an attendant was so easy that I had a full grasp of it after only a few hours of training. But, even that straightforward work taught me how to distinguish between important and non-important data.

었다. 남자는 벤치에 나와 앉아 있었고 담배를 피우고 있었다.

전 약속이 있어서 빨리 가야 해요. 오늘은 전보다 두 배는 주셔야 해요. 이 명단은 모두 진짜배기라서…….

좀 성급했던 건 사실이었다. 남자는 삐딱하게 고개를 든 채 내 얼굴을 빤히 올려다보았다. 그리고 담배꽁초를 땅바닥에 내동댕이치며 벌떡 일어섰다.

뭐가 어째! 두 배? 이게 아주 사람을 놀려!

아주 사람을 칠 기세였다.

왜 이러세요.

왜 이래? 너 나한테 준 명단이 얼마나 삼류인지 알기나 해? 대부분 주소가 틀려서 찾을 수가 없어. 직장을 옮겼거나 그만둔 것들이 더 많다구. 게다가 죽은 것들은 또 왜 그렇게 많아. 너 삼류지? 내가 너 같은 삼류하고 거래를 했다는 게 창피스럽다. 너 다시는 이 바닥에 발 들여놓을 생각 마. 너 인생이 불쌍해서 봐주는 거야.

그리고 침묵. 남자는 씩씩거리며 나를 노려보며 서 있었고 나는 아무 말도 하지 못하고 당하고 있었다. 그럼 받은 돈을 되돌려 달라는 건가, 아니면 남은 명단을 그냥 달라는 것인가, 남자에게 할 말을 준비해야 했지만

I took the files on a Saturday. The previous Friday evening, there was a farewell party for me and I was planning to pack a little that Saturday afternoon. In the office that day, the only staff members on duty were dozing off, leaning far back into their chairs. Nobody came to me or checked on me. I took my toothbrush, hand mirror, health insurance card, and the detailed statements of my salary and packed them into my bag. And then, I turned on my computer like always. As I tidied up, I looked at the files I'd managed with a lengthy list of passwords. Once, they'd seemed so important and now they suddenly didn't even look worth keeping at all. I erased all of them. Then, I opened the membership information files that I'd managed for so long through phone calls, postcards, and emails, and I felt sad. I felt like keeping them as evidence that I'd worked here for ten years. After saying good-bye to the office's sleeping clerk, I left and went to the snack bar where I used to go with the other female office clerks. I ate a very spicy *tteokbokgi*, crushing the hard-boiled egg with my fork. I was about to leave after finishing when the waitress called me. I thought she might have recognized me as a regular and wanted to say good-bye, but she just wanted

속사포처럼 쏟아내는 통에 남자의 말 중간에 끼어들 틈이 없었다. 남자는 조심해, 라고 말하고는 한참 노려보다가 휘적휘적 공원을 걸어 지하철역 쪽으로 갔다. 그렇지 않다고, 내가 했던 일이 그렇게 형편없는 건 아니었다고, 난 그렇게 형편없는 사람이 아니라고, 금방이라도 남자를 따라잡을 기세로 몇 걸음 달렸지만 이내 그 자리에 멈추어 서고 말았다.

나는 남자에게 넘기지 않은 마지막 파일이 담긴 디스켓을 책상 속 깊숙이 넣어두고는 며칠간 몸살을 앓았다. 어느새 고속도로 주변에도 짙은 녹음이 들고 있었다. 먼지를 뒤집어쓰긴 했지만 언덕진 곳마다 들꽃도 피었다. 변함없이 밥을 짓고 고요한 밥상을 놓고 아버지와 마주 대하는 날이 변함없이 이어졌다.

아버지 무슨 생각해요?

아버지는 수저 위에 올려주는 생선살을 말없이 입 속으로 들여간다.

아무 생각도 안 해.

아버지 옛날에 좋아하던 여자 생각해요?

아버지는 수저를 내려놓고는 방으로 들어가 텔레비전을 켠다. 아버지와 나의 대화는 언제나 이런 식이다.

to let me know I had red pepper stain on the chest area of my top.

The man called again. He said he wanted to buy the list of that last two thousand people. I didn't expect him to call again after the last transaction. I wanted to do this last transaction more shrewdly than I had before. It was evening. I went to Jang-chungdan Park as the man suggested. I'd never been there before. There weren't many people around. There was only the sound of tennis balls from the tennis courts nearby. The man was sitting on a bench smoking.

"I have to leave early. I have an appointment. You have to pay double today. This list is the real thing..."

It was true that I was rushing a little. The man looked up at me obliquely and stared. Then, he threw his cigarette to the ground and shot to his feet.

"What the hell are you talking about? Double? You think I'm some kind of idiot?"

He looked ready to hit me.

"What's wrong?" I steeled myself.

"What's wrong? Do you know how third-rate the lists you gave me were? Most of the addresses you

그러고 보니 아버지의 나이가 팔십에 가까웠다. 일본으로 만주로 안 가본 데 없이 다 다니면서 수없이 많은 자식들을 낳았다고 했지만 지금의 아버지는 고요함을 벗삼아 산다. 그 많다던 자식들은 다 어디로 갔는지 모르겠다. 혹시 내가 아버지의 손녀인 것은 아닐까 생각한 적이 있다. 아버지의 자식들 중 하나가 맡겨두었다가 찾아가지 않아 할아버지의 차지가 되었고, 이제는 할아버지를 아버지처럼 모시고 사는, 악다구니를 쓸 일도 없이 그저 동거인처럼 사는 손녀 말이다.

내년 봄 오기 전에 이 동네서 이사 가요.

텔레비전을 보고 있는 아버지 방 쪽에 대고 다짐하듯 말한다.

난 여기도 좋아.

아버지 꽃 좋아하죠? 아버지 좋아하는 꽃 많이 피는 곳으로 가요.

아버지는 대답이 없다. 몸살 끝이라 입 속에서는 단내가 나고, 더위가 시작되려는지 후텁지근한 기운이 감돈다. 방바닥에 누워 온몸을 가능한 한 바닥에 밀착시킨다. 이런 자세로 호흡을 하는 것이 마음을 진정시키는 데 도움이 된다. 남자에게 넘긴 그 명단들은 어떻게 된

gave me were so wrong that we couldn't locate them at all. More people changed their workplaces and quit their jobs than not. And how come so many of them were dead? Your information was third-rate and you knew it, right? I'm ashamed to have traded with you. Don't even think about coming back to this field again. I'm being generous because I take pity on you."

Then, silence. The man was glaring at me, panting, and I just stood there, unable to respond. So, did he want me to refund him? Or, was he asking me to hand him the rest of the list for free? I should have prepared a response, but I couldn't find a moment to interrupt his torrent of complaints.

"Watch yourself!"

He continued to glare at me before walking across the park towards the subway station, swinging his arms dramatically.

"I didn't make such a pathetic transaction. I'm not such a pathetic person," I muttered under my breath and ran after him as if I could quickly catch up to him, but I stopped shortly into my pursuit.

After deciding to keep the diskette of the last file I hadn't handed the man deep in my desk drawer, I

것일까. 수많은 이름들이 그렇게 아무 쓸모도 없다는 게 믿어지지 않지만 모든 게 순식간에 변하는 게 사실이다. 나는 오래전의 그 명단을 이제서야 유통시킨 셈이었으니까.

트럭이었다. 육중한 물체가 미끄러져 안전하게 정지하는 소리였다. 트럭이 온 것이 틀림없었다. 어지럼증이 일었다. 밤 고양이들이 트럭 주변을 맴돌았다. 트럭은 좀 지쳐 보였다. 고무 타이어는 허옇게 먼지를 쓰고 있었다. 남자는 시동을 끄고 트럭에서 내렸다. 남자의 커다란 몸이 내 앞을 가로막았다. 남자는 청바지 주머니에서 담배를 꺼내 물고는 라이터를 켰다. 그렇게 크고 파란 라이터 불꽃은 처음 보았다.

어디서 오는 길이죠? 이 트럭은 달리지 않나요?

남자는 트럭 앞 범퍼를 쓰다듬으며 중얼거리는 자기 키 반만큼 작은 여자를 한동안 쳐다보기만 하더니, 손에 든 담배를 내던지고는 나를 가볍게 들어올려 조수석으로 밀어넣는다. 남자가 차에 올라탄다. 남자가 어찌나 큰지 트럭이 잠깐 쿨렁댄다. 남자는 백미러를 쳐다보며 짧은 머리칼을 애써 한 손에 잡아 한 방향으로 빗어넘긴다. 남자의 다음 동작은 트럭의 시동을 켜는 일

lay sick in bed for several days. In the meantime, the trees around the highway turned greener. I cooked rice and quietly sat across the table with Father as usual.

"What are you thinking about, Father?"

Father brings the piece of fish that I carefully placed in his spoon to his mouth.

"I don't think."

"Are you thinking of the woman you liked when you were young?"

In response, Father puts his spoon down on the table and leaves for the other room to turn on the TV. Our conversations are always like this. Come to think of it, he is almost eighty now. Although I heard that he travelled everywhere, to Japan and to Manchuria, and had children all over, by the way Father lives these days solitude appears to be his only friend now. I wonder where all of his many children are now. I once wondered if I wasn't his granddaughter. A granddaughter one of his children entrusted him with and never reclaimed, so ended up with him and lived with him as if he was my father. A granddaughter who doesn't have to struggle with him, but just lives like a roommate.

"Let's move out of this neighborhood before next

이다. 남자의 부드러운 손등에 가려져 자동차 키는 보이지 않는다. 대신 부드러운 엔진음을 내며 트럭이 움직이기 시작한다. 트럭이 길가로 방향을 틀려는 순간, 나는 막 핸들을 돌리려는 남자의 팔을 잡았다. 그리고는 아버지가 누워 있는 집을 복잡한 기분으로 쳐다봤다.

트럭은 쉬지 않고 달렸다. 남자가 틀어놓은 라디오는 가는 지역에 따라 주파수가 맞지 않아 수시로 지직거렸다. 달리다가 갈림길을 만나면 남자는 손가락을 들어 어느 쪽으로 달려야 할지를 물었고, 나는 느낌에 따라 선지자처럼 길을 택했다. 남자는 앞만 보고 달렸다. 남자의 오른쪽 뺨에는 여드름 자국이 있었는데 무심히 앞만 보고 달리는 그의 표정이 좀 바보스러웠다. 한참을 달리던 트럭은 새벽 해안도로를 따라 속력을 늦췄다. 내가 한 일이라고는 트럭이 인도하는 곳에 닿을 때마다 눈앞에 펼쳐지는 풍경을 고스란히 마음속에 담아두는 것뿐이었다. 하얗게 빛나는 아침 자갈길 위를 달리기도 했는데, 울퉁불퉁한 길 위를 달리면서도 엉덩이를 아프게 하지 않을 만큼 남자의 운전 솜씨는 유연했다.

트럭이 다시 수많은 표지판과 가로등이 서 있는 고속

spring," I say to Father watching TV, as if promising him.

"I like it here, too."

"You like flowers, don't you? Let's move to a place where there are lots of flowers."

No answer from Father. There's a stuffy taste in my mouth because of a few days' illness I'm recovering from. It feels somewhat muggy, perhaps because the hot weather is about to begin. Lying on the floor, I try to lie as flat as possible. Breathing from this position helps me calm down. Although I can't believe all those names became useless, it is true that everything changes instantly. The list I'm circulating now was a pretty old one.

The sound of a truck. The sound of a heavy object sliding in and safely coming to a halt. There is no doubt that the truck has come. I feel dizzy. Night cats circle around the truck. The truck looks a little worn out. The rubber tires are covered with gray dust. The engine turns off and the man gets out from the truck. His large body blocks my vision. He takes a cigarette out of his jean pants pocket and lights it. I have never seen such a large, blue flame.

"Where are you coming from? Doesn't this truck

도로를 달리게 되었을 때는 출발한 지 하루가 지난 후였다. 트럭은 또 국도를 달렸다. 다시 또 고속도로에서 국도. 남자는 국도 주변의 비닐하우스 무밭에서 이제 막 살집이 잡혀가는 무를 뽑아 손수 껍질을 벗겨주기도 했고, 지저분한 속옷이 가득 들었다는 가방 속에서 눅신해진 초콜릿을 꺼내주기도 했다. 게다가 기름을 넣기 위해 들른 주유소에서는 사람들이 모여 나눠 먹던 붉은 간 몇 점과 질긴 처녑도 얻어왔다. 내가 남자의 입에 넣어주려던 간 조각이 열어놓은 창문으로 들어온 바람에 날려 남자의 뺨에 붙어버렸다. 우리는 천치들처럼 웃었다. 낮이든 밤이든 졸릴 때 조금씩 자고, 먹고 싶을 때 조금씩 먹었다. 피곤하지도 배고프지도 않은 신기한 여행이었다.

트럭이 나를 내려놓은 곳은 자동차 바퀴 자국만 어지럽게 중앙에 그려져 있는 벌판 한가운데였다. 누런 황토색 벌판 저만치에 목덜미 갈기와 꼬리가 푸른색인 말들이 느릿느릿 오가고 있었다. 트럭은 시동을 끄고도 엔진 소리가 쿨룩거렸다. 너무 오래 달린 탓이었다. 남자는 시동을 끄자마자 곯아떨어졌다. 나는 감각을 잃은 두 다리에 겨우 힘을 주었다. 저만치 집들이 보였다. 눈

run?" I mutter and then pat the bumper of the car.

After staring at me for a while, a woman half as tall as himself, he throws his cigarette down on to the ground and lightly scoops me up and into the passenger seat. The man gets back into the truck. He is so big the truck sags and trembles briefly. He looks into the rearview mirror and tries to comb his short hair to one side. Then he starts the engine.

I can't see the key because the back of his large, soft hand blocks my view. Instead, the truck begins to inch forward as the engine purrs. The moment the truck is about to turn to the curb, I catch his arm. Then, I look back at the house where Father is lying down. My feelings are complicated.

The truck ran without pause. The radio frequently turned to static because our radio frequency changed from location to location. Whenever we ran into a fork, he asked me which way we should go by indicating with his finger, and I'd choose one based on how I felt as if I was some sort of prophet. The man only looked ahead as he drove. There were traces of pimples on his right cheek. He drove the truck forward for miles and miles and I

에 보이기는 해도 가까운 거리가 아니었다. 집이 가까워지면 가까워질수록 발걸음이 느려졌다.

한 집에서 여자가 창틀에 턱을 괴고 벌판을 내다보고 있었다. 여자는 늘어뜨린 긴 머리를 두 손으로 만지고 있었는데 뽀얀 먼지 속에 서 있는 나를 발견하고는, 대문을 열고 집 밖으로 나왔다. 그리고 눈을 가늘게 뜨고 나를 쳐다봤다. 그리고 가까이 와 내 얼굴과 손, 가슴과 등을 쓰다듬기 시작했는데 그 손길에 많은 얘기가 들어 있는 것만 같았다. 여자가 나를 두 팔로 지그시 안아주었는데 여자의 몸에서는 물비린내가 났다. 공교롭게도 여자와 나는 키가 똑같았다.

여자는 집에서 긴 고무호스를 가지고 나와 집 앞 벌판에서 쌀을 씻어 밥을 지었다. 트럭은 그때까지도 꿈쩍없이 자고 있었고 밥 냄새가 벌판에 퍼져나갈 때쯤이 되어서야 깨어났다. 남자는 집 앞으로 트럭을 몰고 와 라디오를 틀었고 라이트를 켰다. 여자는 집 안에서 전깃줄에 매달린 전구 소켓을 가지고 나왔고 알전구를 끼워 대문 앞에 매달았다. 흰 밥 위에 올려진 반찬은 마른 장작불 위에 석쇠를 얹어 구운 개구리 뒷다리였다. 벌판 어디에서 개구리가 났을까 궁금했지만 남자와 내게

thought he suddenly looked a bit stupid. After a while, the truck slowed down along the west coast. Wherever the truck led us, I tried to preserve the scenery in my mind. The man's driving was so skillful that I never felt any pain in my rear, even when we drove over gravel roads.

It was the day after we started that we entered the highway with its many signposts and streetlamps. Then truck pulled back to the local road. Again to highway, and then, to the local road. The man pulled a just-fattening turnip from out a greenhouse turnip field along one of the local roads. He also gave me a softened chocolate bar that he took out of his bag full of dirty laundry. He once got a few pieces of bloody liver and the chewy psalterium people were sharing from a gas station where we dropped by to fill the gas tank. Blown away by some wind from the truck's open window, a piece of liver I tried to feed him stuck to his cheek. We laughed like idiots. It was an interesting way of traveling; we slept a little whenever we felt sleepy whether it was day or night, and ate a little whenever we felt hungry. It was the kind of trip where we never felt tired or hungry.

The truck dropped me off in the middle of a field

끊임없이 밥숟갈을 물려주는 여자 때문에 물어볼 수가 없었다. 우리가 피운 불빛에 검고 마른 벌판이 타버릴 것만 같았다.

밥을 먹고 여자와 나는 집 안으로 들어가 창틀에 걸터앉았고, 남자는 약속이나 한 듯이 어릴 적부터 화가가 꿈이었다면서 트럭에서 가져온 냉동연어 상자 위에 여자와 나를 그리기 시작했다. 남자가 그린 그림은 도무지 누가 누구인지 알 수 없게 되어 있어서 우리를 웃게 만들었는데, 밤하늘을 날다 잠깐씩 트럭 위에 와 앉아 있다 날아가곤 하던 새들만큼은 크고 분명하게 그렸다.

밤이 깊어갔고, 트럭은 꼭 밤에 떠나야 한다고 했다. 여자는 내가 벌판을 걸어 집 앞에 도착했을 때보다 더욱 따뜻하게 나를 안아주었고, 내 손바닥 안에 자신의 긴 머리를 묶었던 오색실과 누구의 것인지 모를 이빨이 담긴 유리병을 선물로 주었다. 트럭이 달리는 동안 나는 여자가 내게 준 선물을 가슴에 꼭 안고 있었다.

나는 남자에게 고맙다는 인사를 하고 싶어서 핸들을 잡지 않은 남자의 한 손에 내 비밀의 징표인 마지막 디스켓을 쥐어주었다. 남자는 신기한 물건이라는 듯 훑어보고는 운전석 발밑에 아무렇게나 던져버렸다. 하지만

where there were only crisscrossing tire tracks. Horses with blue manes and tails strolled along a little ways away in an ocher field. After the engine turned off, the truck still coughed and sputtered. It had been driven too long. As soon as he turned the engine off, the man fell fast asleep. I could barely manage to stand; my legs had lost all sensation. I could see houses far away. Although I could see them, they were not so close to where I was. The nearer I got to the houses, the slower I walked.

A woman in one of the houses was looking out across the field, her chin propped up along a windowsill. She was combing her long hair with her fingers. When she saw me stand in the midst of thick dust, she opened the door and came out of her house. Then, she squinted her eyes and stared at me. She came up to me and began to stroke my face, hands, chest, and back. Her hands seemed to carry many stories. The woman hugged me gently, and I could smell the slight scent of fish that I'd sometimes noticed in water. Incidentally, she and I were the same height.

The woman brought a long hose out from her house and, after washing some rice in the field in front of her house, cooked some of it for me. The

나는 비밀을 고백했다는 사실만으로도 마음이 편안해졌다. 얼마를 달렸을까. 남자는 혼자서 중얼거리고 있었다.

내가 본 여자 중에 당신이 제일 못생겼어요.

남자는 웃으면서 라디오 볼륨을 높였다. 그 어느 때보다도 깨끗한 전파 상태로 유행가가 흘러나왔고 남자는 침을 튀기며 노래를 따라 불렀다. 하늘 위의 흐린 별빛은 끈질기게 반짝거리고 있었다.

트럭은 그날 밤 이후 움직이지 않았다. 밤이고 낮이고 트럭은 서 있기만 했고 남자의 움직임도 없었다. 어느 날 새벽, 트럭이 도난 차량이었음이 밝혀졌다. 그날 새벽에 청소차를 쫓아가던 남자가 죽었다. 청소차만 보면 흥분해 슬리퍼를 신고 두 발을 질질 끌며 따라 뛰던 남자는 안개 때문에 뒤를 보지 못하고 후진하던 청소차에 치여 죽었다. 그는 차에 치인 순간에도 웃고 있었다고 한다. 다들 미친놈이라고 부르는, 청소차를 쫓아다니기 이전의 그의 최초의 이름은 무엇이었을까.

청소차 사고를 수사하러 나온 경찰 두 명이 트럭을 수상히 여겼다. 그러고 보니 트럭은 번호판도 보이지

truck was still sleeping. It awoke about the time when the smell of cooked rice spread all over the field. The man drove his truck to the front of the house and turned on the radio and the lights. The woman brought sockets for some light bulbs from out of her house and screwed in the bulbs and hung them in front of her door. The side dishes on the rice were frog legs grilled over a wood fire. I wondered where she found those frogs in this field, but I couldn't ask her because she kept on pushing spoonfuls of rice into our mouths. The fire we'd made seemed to burn the dark, dry field.

After eating, the woman and I entered the house and sat in front of the windowsill, and then the man began to draw us on the surface of the box of frozen salmon he took out from the truck. He said that his childhood dream was to become an artist. Because we couldn't tell who was who in his picture, we laughed, but he drew the birds that sometimes briefly alighted the truck very clearly, and very largely.

The night was deepening, and the man said the truck must leave at night. The woman gave me a hug, an even warmer one than that she had given me when I'd arrived. She placed in my palm several

않을 만큼 지저분했다. 트럭 안에서 수상한 물건이 발견되지는 않은 것 같았다. 최소한 운전석에서는 그랬다. 경찰 한 사람은 들고 있던 방망이로 트럭 뒤칸, 굳게 잠긴 은색 컨테이너를 두드렸다. 야, 이 안에 뭐 있을까? 남은 경찰 한 사람이 경찰차로 돌아가 전화를 걸었다. 얼마 후 한 남자가 왔다. 열쇠 수리공이었다. 수리공은 알루미늄 사다리를 트럭 뒤에 기대어놓고 올라가 굳게 잠긴 짐칸의 문을 열기 시작했다. 문은 생각보다 아주 쉽게 열렸다. 경찰 두 사람과 열쇠 수리공 그리고 나까지 모두 네 사람이 트럭 안을 들여다봤다. 텅 비어 있었다. 아니 빛 때문에 일시적으로 비어 보였다. 원숭이였다. 황색 털에, 불쾌한 냄새에, 그저 눈만 동그랗게 뜬 원숭이가 사람들보다 더 놀란 얼굴로 마구 쏟아져 들어오는 햇볕에 순식간에 노출되었다. 형체도 없이 일그러진 채 말라붙어버린 두툼한 종이 박스 더미 위에 앉아 있던 원숭이는 자리에서 일어나 움직이다가 갑자기 잔뜩 겁먹은 눈빛이 되어 동작을 멈췄다. 어디서 왔는지, 어디에서 태어났는지, 왜 깜깜한 트럭 짐칸에 묶여 있는지 알 수 없는 원숭이의 눈빛이 불안하게 떨렸다. 원숭이는 긴 팔을 움직여 자꾸 어딘가를 가리켰다. 그곳

colorful strings, which she had used to tie her long hair, and a glass jar, which had an unknown person's tooth in it. As the truck began to inch forward, I held those gifts tight in my arms.

I wanted to thank the man, so I handed him the last diskette, the last sign of my secret. He looked at it as if it was something mysterious, then he tossed it onto the floor of the truck. But I felt relieved that I'd confessed my secret to someone. How far had we traveled? The man muttered something to himself.

"You're the ugliest woman I've ever seen."

The man smiled and then turned up the volume on the radio. A single clean wave of a popular song, cleaner than any I'd ever heard before, flowed out from the radio and the man began to sing along, spattering saliva all over as he sang. The stars were sparkled dimly and persistently in the sky.

The truck never moved after that day. It just stood there day and night and the man was never seen moving around, either. One day, at dawn, it was discovered that the truck was a stolen vehicle. That same dawn, a man who'd always been excited to see the garbage truck and would run after it

은 자동차가 달리는 고속도로였고, 원숭이는 끵끵끵 소리를 내며 자신을 쳐다보고 있는 사람들 중 누군가와 눈길을 마주치려 했다. 나는 원숭이의 눈을 피해 몸을 돌렸다. 야, 이거 가짜 번호판도 수십 개야. 사시미칼도 두 세트나 있어. 경찰 한 사람이 가까이 다가왔다. 이봐요, 이 트럭 본 적 있어요? 경찰이 내게 물었지만 못 들은 척 집 쪽으로 달렸다. 먼지 묻은 나뭇잎 하나가 날아와 가슴 위에 떨어졌다.

『흔들리다』, 문학동네, 2002

died. The man was run over by a garbage truck backing out as he ran after it, dragging his slippers. The truck driver hadn't been able to see him because of fog. People said that he'd been smiling the entire time, even at the moment the truck ran him over. What had people called him before he'd begun to follow the garbage truck, this man everyone just called crazy?

Two police officers came to investigate the garbage truck accident and thought the truck looked suspicious. Come to think of it, the truck was so dirty you couldn't even see its license plate. It seemed that no suspicious objects were found inside. At least, nothing suspicious from the driver's seat. A police officer tapped the truck's securely locked trailer. *Hey, what do you think is inside of this?* The other police officer returned to their patrol car and made a phone call. Soon, a man arrived. He was a locksmith. The locksmith leaned an aluminum ladder against the rear of the truck, went up the ladder, and began to pick the securely fastened truck door. The door opened easier than expected. The two police officers, the locksmith, and I looked inside the trailer. It was empty. No, it looked empty just for a moment because of the light. There was a monkey inside. A monkey, covered in brown hair, reeking, and wide-eyed, suddenly revealed itself. Exposed to the sunlight pouring ruthlessly inside, it looked more surprised than us human beings now looking at him. The monkey stood up from the crushed and desiccated cardboard box it had been perched on and began to move around until it suddenly stopped, its eyes full of fear. The eyes of this monkey, of which we knew nothing of where it had come from, where it had been born, and why it'd been tied up inside this dark trailer, trembled nervously. The monkey raised its long arm and pointed to some place, and then pointed again and again. It was pointing in the direction of the highway where the cars roared by. The monkey trilled and chirped nervously, trying desperately to make eye contact with one of us as we just stared at it. Avoiding its eyes, I try to hide myself. *Hey, look here! There are dozens of stolen license plates! My, there are even two sets of sashimi knives!* A police officer came up to me. *Hey, Miss, have you seen this truck before?* I pretended not to hear him and I began to run in the direction of home. A dirt-streaked leaf flew and landed on my chest.

Translated by Jeon Seung-hee

해설

Afterword

환각의 치유 효과

황현경 (문학평론가)

세기말을 통과한 한국 소설은 다양한 장르적 문법들을 활발히 차용하며 시야를 넓혀가던 가운데에 마침내 '무중력 공간'이라는 새로운 영역과 맞닥뜨리게 되었다. 이 미지의 영역에 대해 적극적으로 개척한 성과 중 하나는 바로 '환상'의 (재)발견이라 할 수 있다. 환상이라는 무한에 가까운 지평을 막 열어젖힌 새로운 세기의 작가들은 그 신대륙을 마음껏 누비고 다녔다. 결과물을 놓고 벌어진 문학의 정치성 측면에서의 치열한 검증은 아직도 진행 중이지만, 그와는 별개로 이들 작가들로 인하여 한국 소설의 외연이 확장되었다는 것만큼은 그대로 인정하지 않을 수 없는 사실이다.

The Healing Effect of Hallucination

Hwang Hyeon-gyeong (literary critic)

As it passes through the turn of the century even as it expands its scope into the widely experimental field of genre, Korean fiction has finally come to a zero gravity space. One of these achievements of this active exploration into this unknown domain has the discovery, or perhaps rediscovery of fantasy. Korean writers of our new century, who have just come up the new, almost infinite horizon of fantasy, have begun to explore this new continent freely. Although a fierce examination of their products' political characters are still underway, it is undeniable that these writers have expanded the fictional territory of Korea, no matter how unclear it is

강영숙은 그 개척자들 중 한 명이며, 여전히 그곳에서 아직 발길이 닿지 않은 곳을 부지런히 찾아다니는 중이다. 이러한 맥락에서 초기작이 묶인 첫 소설집『흔들리다』(2002)는 작가의 소설 세계 전반을 미리 압축된 형태로 제시한 출사표였다 해도 과언이 아니다. 여기에는 현실과 환상이 끝내 그 경계조차 구분하기 힘들 만큼 자연스럽게 뒤섞인 작품들이 수록되어 있다. 그중에서도「트럭」은 개별 단편으로서의 밀도가 높기도 하거니와, 소설집 전체, 나아가 작가의 소설적 관심과 지향을 대표하기에 손색이 없다는 점에서 단연 문제적인 작품이다.

구분 자체가 무의미한 것이라 할지라도,「트럭」의 백미인 환상 장면들을 충분히 음미하기 위해 먼저 전체 이야기가 뿌리를 두고 있는 현실 장면들을 꼼꼼히 살필 필요가 있다. 소설은 과거 사무 보조원으로 꼭 십 년 동안 근무했던 회사를 퇴직한 여주인공 '나'의 시점으로 진행된다. '나'는 회사를 그만두면서 "십 년을 일했다는 증거로 그냥 가지고 있고 싶었다"며 가지고 나온 육천 명의 회원 정보가 담긴 파일을 세 번에 걸쳐 정체불명의 남자에게 팔아넘긴다. 이 과정에서 작가는 '나'의 복

as to what conclusions these new examination will lead to.

Kang Young-sook, one of those pioneers in the domain of fantasy, is still diligently exploring the untrod corners of this new continent. In this sense, her first short story collection, *Shaken* (2002), has been a compact announcement of her fictional world to come. *Shaken* contains stories where reality and fantasy are mixed so seamlessly that it becomes almost impossible to distinguish one from the other. Among these exhilarating, disorienting new stories, "Truck" stands out because of its dense structure and exceptional quality representative of the work as whole. Furthermore, the direction of the author's overall fictional interest intrigues a wide range of audiences.

Although distinguishing fantasy from reality in this story might be pointless, it is necessary to study the more grounded, conventionally realistic scenes, the basis of the story, in order to fully appreciate the outstanding quality of the story's more fantastical elements. This short story follows the point of view of a nameless narrator who has retired from the company where she has worked as an attendant for ten years. As the story begins, we learn

잡 미묘한 심리를 민감하게 포착하여 제시하고 있다.

당연하다는 듯 이 모든 사건의 공간적 배경은 서울이다. 이미 첫 장면에서부터 황사 바람이 불어닥치는 이곳은 서로가 서로를 모르는 채 살아가는 삭막한 공간이다. '나'는 파일을 받아가는 남자가 누구인지 모르며 그와 어떻게 마주하게 되었는지도 모른다. 또한 이곳은 청소차만 보면 흥분해 슬리퍼 바람으로 따라가곤 하던 한 사내의 죽음에 직면해 누구 하나 그 이유도 그의 이름도 모르는 곳이다. 이렇듯 황폐한 대도시에서 소갈증에 걸린 듯 냉수를 거푸 들이켜며 모르는 이들의 이름을 모르는 이에게 넘기는 '나'가 있고, 그 맞은편에 언젠가 어딘가에서 흰 아까시나무 꽃잎을 잔뜩 묻히고 들어온 아버지와, '나'의 환상 속에 나타나 어딘지 모를 곳에서 연못에 몸을 담그는 혹 '나'인지도 모를 여자가 있다.

그리고 이 먼지 가득한 도시에, 화려한 은색으로 반짝이는 트럭과 쿰쿰한 땀냄새를 풍기며 트럭을 보살피는 남자가 있다. 이 봄밤의 트럭은 환한 불빛으로 꽃가루를 춤추게 하며, 그 마술적인 힘으로 "식물성과 광물성의 우연한 어울림"을 불러일으키는 신비한 존재이다. '나'는 멈추어 있어도 달리는 것만 같던 그 트럭을 타고

that she has already sold the member information file, which she took when she retired for the mere fact that she "felt like keeping them as evidence" as proof of her work for the past ten years. As the narrator exchanges this information to an unidentified man over three tense meetings, the author deftly captures the narrator's complex and delicate psychology.

The backdrop of *Shaken* is contemporary Seoul, a bleak landscape for several reasons., The city is swept by yellow dust and populated by citizens who barely know each other. The narrator herself knows neither the identity of the man purchasing the files from her nor how he ended up becoming her counterpart in this transaction. Additionally, Kang's Seoul is the sort of place where a man perpetually wearing slippers and aimlessly pursuing garbage trucks is killed one day, and nobody knows how he died or who he was. In the center of this desolate metropolis, there is the narrator: she constantly drinks cold water like someone suffering from un unquenchable thirst and sells the names of people she doesn't know to a man whose name she also doesn't know. But, on the other hand, there is also her father, who one day came

피곤한지도 배고픈지도 모르게 달려 '나'인지 모를 환상 속 여자와 만난다. 결말에 밝혀지는 바, 모든 게 다 실려 있던 트럭에는 사실 가짜 번호판 수십 개와 사시미칼 두 세트만 실려 있을 뿐. 그러니 어딘가 모르게 비현실적이었던 이 여정은 역시 '나'의 환상이었다고 해야 하겠다. 트럭이 뿜어내는 그 기묘한 아름다움이 이 삭막한 도시 한가운데에서 '정말'로 가능할 리가 있겠는가.

그렇다면 그 환상의 정체는 무엇인가. 그것은 수많은 이들의 이름이 아무 의미도 없는 이곳에서 병들어간 '나'의 마음이 만들어낸 허상이다. 그 환각 속에서만 '나'는 트럭을 운전하는 남자에게 회원 정보가 담긴 디스켓을 건네며 그 무의미한 이름들로부터 온전히 벗어나 자유로워진다. 이것뿐이라면 그저 현실 도피에 불과할 터, 하나 '나'의 그 충만한 마음이 마주한 게 다름 아닌 '나' 자신 아니던가. 그렇게 도플갱어와 대면하고 나서야 비로소 '나'는 고유명을 얻는다. 트럭을 운전하는 남자의 "내가 본 여자 중에 당신이 제일 못생겼"다는 중얼거림을 통해서 말이다. 그렇기에 이는 마침내 스스로와 정직하게 대면하기 위한 아름다운 여정이다.

하여 이러한 환상은 지극히 개인적인 동시에 주체적

home with clothes full of petals, and a nameless woman, who takes a dip in a nearby pond in the narrator's fantasy and who might be the narrator herself.

Additionally, the final central figure in Kang's story is the silvery shiny truck and a man covered in a sour sweat smell who takes care of that truck in this city replete with dust. This truck that appears on a random spring night is a mysterious being that makes pollens dance in its bright light and enables "the sudden union of plant and mineral." The narrator decides to board this truck, where she is neither weary nor hungry and eventually comes to meet the woman in fantasy. In the conclusion of the story, it turns out that there are only dozens of stolen license plates and two sets of sashimi knives in this truck instead of her earlier perception that "there's everything inside this truck." Thus, this rather surreal journey proves to be the narrator's fantasy. That strange beauty that the narrator perceives emanates from this truck wouldn't have "really" been possible in the midst of this bleak metropolis, would it?

What is the meaning of this fantasy, then? It is an illusion created by the narrator sick of a place

이라는 의미에서 엄밀히 말해 환각이라 해야 옳다. 환각이기에 그것은 일차적으로는 병증이지만, 결과적으로는 그 환각의 과정이 자아와의 대면을 위함이라는 점에서 그것을 그대로 자기 치유의 과정이라 해도 좋으리라. 치유의 결과로 '나'가 대면하게 되는 것이 하필 '제일 못생긴' 저 자신의 '몸'이라는 것. 누차 지적되었듯 이러한 성찰은 문학적 사유의 매개체로 여성의 몸을 활발하게 활용할 줄 아는 이 작가가 수시로 도달하곤 하는 매우 독특한 지점이다.

환각을 통과해 소설은 의미심장한 결말로 향한다. '나'와 만나고 돌아온 그날 밤 이후부터, 아니 어쩌면 애초부터 단 한 번도 움직이지 않은 트럭의 정체가 밝혀지는 장면에서 소설은 다시 급커브를 돌아 현실에 급정거한다. 거기서 '나'는 결코 이곳을 벗어나지 못하는 또 다른 '나', 황색 털의 원숭이와 대면한다. 트럭을 타고 떠나 만난 그곳의 '나'도, 불쾌한 냄새를 뿜어내는 이곳의 원숭이도 모두 '나'일 진대, 이곳에서 만날 수 있는 '나'는 불안하게 끵끵거리는 원숭이일 뿐이라는 것. 이 장면에 이르러 소설의 명암은 더욱 뚜렷해진다.

병든 이, 그리고 그를 병들게 하는 병든 현실. 「트럭」의

where so many names have no significance at all. It is only in her hallucination where she can hand the diskette containing the membership information to the truck driver and free herself from those insignificant names. However, if this were all of it, the narrator's dream would have been a simple escape from reality. But the narrator confronts her own self in her free state. Only after confronting her doppelgänger does the narrator finally gains her proper name; the truck driver mutters, "You're the ugliest woman I've ever seen." This fantastic journey becomes a beautiful journey where the narrator can finally come face to face with her honest self.

Strictly speaking, then, this fantasy should more accurately be referred to as hallucination in the sense that it is both extremely personal and subjective. And as a hallucination, one might say that it is primarily a symptom of a psychological disorder. By the story's end, however, it is also a process of self-healing because it allows one to confront oneself. The fact that the narrator confronts her "body" that she can see is "the ugliest" as a result of her healing one can see, as critics have often pointed out, that this is a unique place arrived at by

이 두 축은 곧 강영숙 소설 전반을 지탱하는 것이라 할 수 있다. 하나 이것은 어쩐지 낯익지 않은가. 어떠한 방식을 취하든지 간에 현실에 대한 인식적 측면을 포기하지 않은 소설이라면 기어이 이르고야 마는 지점이어서 그렇다. 그렇게 강영숙 소설이 마땅하다는 듯 도달한 이 지점은 새로운 세기의 '무중력' 소설을 향한 비판적 시각에 넌지시 반성을 촉구한다. 요컨대 그 어떤 소설도 완전히 다른 별에서 써올 수는 없는 법. 「트럭」은 이 당연한 사실을 가뿐히 증명하고 있다.

an author who actively adopts the female body as a medium for literary reflection.

Through the narrative techniques of fantasy and hallucination, the story advances towards a meaningful ending. On the same night the narrator confronts her own self, in the scene when the interior of the truck that likely hasn't actually moved at all is revealed, the story makes a sharp U-turn and a sudden stop into reality. The narrator confronts another self who can never escape from the here and now, a monkey swathed in thick brown hair. Both the unknown woman and the reeking monkey are mirrors of the narrator, but the cypher that she is able to meet in the here and now is only the monkey trilling and chirping nervously. On this final note, this scene delineates the bright and dark sides of this story more clearly.

A sick individual and a sick reality that compel the narrator's own sickness—these two axes of "Truck" support Kang Young-sook's overall fictional world. Well, isn't this a very familiar formula? Perhaps, this is because all works that refuse to give up on reality, no matter which route they may take, are still bound to arrive at that. The spot where Kang's fiction arrives at almost naturally urges those critical of the "zero gravity" fiction of our new century to re-examine their own stance. No piece of fiction can be written on a completely different planet and brought back to the earth, right? "Truck" rather nimbly proves this obvious fact.

비평의 목소리

Critical Acclaim

특별히 다채롭다는 느낌을 주는 것은 아니지만 남녀간 연애공간을 거의 설정하지 않고도(표면적으로 강영숙 소설에는 '사랑'의 서사가 없다) 강영숙 소설은 상처 입은 존재의 내면을 드러내고 인간의 발견에 이르는 강렬한 무엇을 지니고 있다. 그것은 눈으로 보고 손으로 만질 수 있는 구체적인 결핍에서 비롯하는 상처의 진정성이다. 쉽게 말해, 강영숙 소설의 인물들은 다리를 심하게 절거나 못난 인간으로 무시당하거나 못생겼거나 뚱뚱하거나 무능한 남편으로 인해 삶의 바닥으로 추락해 있다. 그들의 고통은 당연히 자의식을 포함하지만 그 자의식을 바라보는 명백한 실체를 갖고 있다. 고상한 그

Although not particularly colorful and without any apparent stories of love and romance, Kang Young-sook's stories draw readers in intensely by revealing our own wounded insides and rediscovering our humanity. Kang's stories do this through the honesty of their wounds that originate from concrete, visible and tactile deficiencies. Simply put, Kang's characters hit the definite rock bottoms of their lives. They are crippled, ugly, fat, ignored for their incompetence, or because they have incompetent husbands. Naturally, their pain includes a kind of self-consciousness, but there is also a clear substance that causes this self-conscious-

무엇이 아니다. 그 이하일지도 모르나, 사실은 그 이상이다. 그러니 빗어낼 수 없는 것이다. 다분히 몸('육체'와는 구별해야 할 것 같다. 여기서 몸은 정신의 대립항이 아니다)의 그것이다. 쉽게 넘어설 지점이 보이지 않는다. 해서, 「트럭」에서 본 것처럼 환영의 요청은 강영숙 소설의 담담하면서도 강렬한 내적 필연성을 구축한다.

정홍수

그럼에도 불구하고 강영숙은 여성작가이다. 그런데 여성작가이되 관습적인 의미에서의 여성을 배반하는 여성작가이다. 그녀의 소설에 등장하는 여성인물들은 우리가 익숙하게 알고 있는 일반명사 여성과는 많이 다르다. 일단 그녀들은 덩치가 크지만 힘이 세지 않고 무신경하면서도 섬세하다. 강하면서 나약하고 대범하면서 소심하다. 그들은 어떤 특정한 인물 유형에도 속하지 않는 다면체적 존재들이라는 점에서 쉽게 포착하기 어렵다. "이쪽에도 저쪽에도 속하고 싶지 않았고 남자도 여자도 아닌 일종의 중간자가 되고 싶었다"(「자이언트의 시대」)는 작가의 고백은 관습적인 성별 범주에서 벗

ness. This substance is not something noble. It could be something that is far less than noble, but it is, in fact, more vital than simple nobility. Thus, it cannot be something that one simply concocts. It is of body, though not in the sense that it is opposite of mind. We cannot see any place from which we can easily overcome it. Therefore, the demand for illusion becomes a calm, yet strong inner necessity in Kang's fiction as eloquently illustrated in "Truck."

Jeong Hong-su

Despite it all, Kang Young-sook is a female writer. Still, she is a female writer who betrays women in the conventional sense of the word. Her female characters are considerably different from women as we might know well as a common noun. Above all, they are very large, but not as strong and absentminded, yet sensitive. Both strong and weak, magnanimous and timid. They are multifaceted beings, defying easy categorization. The following quote from "The Time When I Was a Giant" illustrates very well the author's desire to think beyond conventional gender categorization: "I wanted to

어나고 싶은 작가의 바람을 잘 보여준다.

심진경

그러니 강영숙이 인공낙원에서 실낙원을 발견하는 것은 오히려 당연하다. 강영숙의 소설이 인공낙원의 풍경에서 오히려 실낙원 혹은 연옥을 발견하는 것은 인공낙원의 풍경이 이미 인간의 통제 범위를 넘어설 정도로 자립화되었다고 판단하기 때문이다. 인공낙원의 풍경은 이제 스스로 쉼없이 만들어내고 유포하는 이미지를 통해 인간에게 있는 그대로의 사실에 접근할 가능성조차 차단하고 또 다양하고 발랄해야 할 축제와 환상체계를 하나의 체계로 환원시키기에 이르렀다는 것이다. 강영숙의 소설에 따르면 인공낙원은 이미 이상적 자아, 혹은 초자아의 직위에까지 올라서서 오히려 인간들의 몸과 정신까지를 규제하는 것은 물론 결과적으로 인간 전체를 기계로 전락시키고 있는 실정이다. 그러니, 강영숙의 소설이 보들레르가 자연적인 것에서 악을 보았듯, 인공적이고 초월적인 것에서 악을 보는 것은 오히려 당연한지도 모르며, 또한 작가 강영숙이 자본주의의 이윤 시스템과 공모한 인공낙원의 풍경이 치밀하게 인

belong to neither this nor that side, and be a sort of middle being between a man and a woman."

Sim Jin-gyeong

Therefore, it is rather natural that Kang Young-sook finds a "paradise lost" in this artificial paradise. Kang finds a lost paradise or purgatory in artificial, paradisiacal scenery because she concludes that this artificial scenery has already traveled beyond the bounds of human control. By continuously creating and distributing images, artificial paradise scenery now blocks the possibility of approaching reality as it is and reduces the diverse and lively festival of fantasy world to a single unified system. In Kang's fictional world, artificial paradise has already acquired the status of an ideal self, a super-ego, not only controlling human bodies and minds, but also degrading all of humanity into a single machine. Thus, it is only natural that Kang sees evil in the artificial and transcendental as Baudelaire saw evil in the natural. Also, Kang's recent interest in the elaborate oppression of human freedom by artificial paradisiacal scenery in collusion with capitalist profit systems is a significant event, not only in

간의 자유를 억압하고 있다는 것에 본격적인 관심을 기울이기 시작했다는 점은 작가 강영숙의 작가적 도정에 있어서도, 그리고 우리 문학 전체를 위해서도 대단히 의미 있는 사건인지도 모른다.

류보선

Kang's literary journey, but also for the sake of Korean literature as a whole.

Ryu Bo-seon

강영숙

강영숙은 1967년 강원도 춘천에서 태어나 14살 때 서울로 이주하기까지 배구나 멀리뛰기 선수로 활동하는 등 주로 운동을 하며 어린 시절을 보냈다. 서울예술대학교에 입학하여 문예창작을 전공했고 교지 편집장을 했다. 1998년 《서울신문》 신춘문예에 단편소설 「팔월의 식사」가 당선되면서 작품 활동을 시작했다.

첫 번째 단편소설집 『흔들리다』(2002)는 그로테스크한 상상력으로 여성의 자의식을 묘사한 작품들로 주목을 받았고, 두 번째 단편소설집 『날마다 축제』(2004)는 자본주의 사회에서 부딪히는 실존적 문제들을 사회적 상상력의 맥락 안에서 다룬 작품들을 선보였다. 세 번째 단편소설집 『빨강 속의 검정에 대하여』(2009)에서는 현대사회를 살아가는 사람들의 관계와 소통의 문제를 무심하고 건조한 문체로 그려냈다. 이 소설집에 실린 「갈색 눈물방울」은 한국문학번역원에서 발행하는 영문 잡지 《리스트(list)》의 '새로운 한국문학 작품' 코너에 영역되어 소개되었고, 역시 같은 작품집에 실린 「해안 없

Kang Young-sook

Born in 1967 in Chuncheon, Gangwon-do, South Korea, Kang Young-sook spent most of her childhood in Chuncheon where she was a varsity volleyball and long jump player until she moved to Seoul at the age of fourteen. In Seoul, her life took a new direction when she began to study creative writing and became the editor-in-chief of the school magazine at the Seoul Institute of the Arts. She made her literary debut in 1998 when she won the *Seoul Shinmun* Spring Literary Contest with the short story, "A Meal in August."

Her first short story collection, *Shaken* (2002), attracted a great deal of critical attention for its depiction of the female consciousness through images of the grotesque. Her second short story collection, *Every Day is a Celebration* (2004), dealt with existential issues in a capitalist society from a broad social context. *Black in Red* (2009) focused its purview on modern social interactions, often presented in a deliberately cool, understated tone. A short story from this collection, "Brown Tears," was

는 바다」는 일본문학잡지인 《분가쿠카이(文學界)》 2010년 10월호에 발표되었다. '도시 누아르' 장르 형식의 영향을 짙게 받은 네 번째 소설집 『아령 하는 밤』은 도시를 부유하는 불안한 영혼들을 그린 작품으로 한국도서관협회 올해의 우수문학도서에 선정되었다. 이 작품집에 실린 단편소설 「문래에서」로 2011년 김유정문학상을 수상했다.

2005년 《문예중앙》에 연재한 장편소설 『리나』는 16살 소녀의 국경 넘기 과정을 형상화한 것으로, 디아스포라와 여성주의적 관점이 포함된 알레고리 소설이자 성장소설이다. 22명의 난민이 'P'라는 이상향의 국가를 향해 국경을 넘는 것으로 시작하는 이 소설에서 그들을 기다리고 있는 것은 숲 속의 화학약품공장, 사막과도 같은 소금들판, 외딴 마을 시링, 창녀촌, 그리고 대규모 공장단지 등이다. 리나는 가는 곳마다 정착해 살아보려고 노력하지만 그러한 시도는 매번 성공하지 못한다. 살인과 강간, 인신매매, 마약밀매, 매춘을 일삼는 온갖 악인들을 만나는 리나의 여정은 현실과 환상이 불분명한, 독특한 블랙 코미디의 방식으로 제시된다. 이 작품은 2006년 한국일보문학상 수상작으로 선정되었다. 이 소

included in the "New Writing From Korea" series in a 2008 issue of, *List: Books from Korea*, a magazine published by the Korea Literature Translation Institute. Additionally, "Ocean without Shore," also from the same collection, was published in the October 2010 issue of *Bungei Shunju*, a Japanese literary magazine. Her fourth short story collection, *The Night He Lifts Weights* (2011), honored with the Korean Library Association Book-of-the-Year Award, was strongly influenced by the urban *noir* genre, depicting the anxieties of mundane city dwellers. A story from this collection, "*From Mullae*," won the 2011 Kim You-jeong Literary Award.

Kang's novel, *Rina* (2006 & 2011), serialized in the quarterly magazine *Literary Joongang* in 2005, was an account of a 16-year-old girl's border-crossing experience, an allegorical diaspora narrative told from a feminist perspective as well as a coming-of-age fable. In the beginning of this novel, twenty-two refugees cross the national border with the hope of finding utopia in the land of P. What awaits them, however, is a chemical plant in the mountains, a desert-like salt field, the isolated village of Siring, a prostitute town, and a large-scale industrial complex. Rina makes several desperate at-

설의 일부는 2010년 하버드대학교에서 발행하는 연간 한국문학전문지 《아젤리아(Azalea)》에 수록되었으며 2011년에 일본의 현대기획실에서 출판되었다. 영어 번역 소설은 2014년 하반기에 출간될 예정이다.

두 번째 장편소설 『라이팅 클럽』은 서울의 북촌(계동)을 배경으로 한 성장소설로 글쓰기에 집착하는 모녀의 갈등과 성장을 담고 있다. 2011년 백신애문학상의 수상작이기도 하며 현재 영어로 번역 중이다. 십대 가출소녀의 일상과 슬픔의 정서를 묘사한 세 번째 장편소설 『슬프고 유쾌한 텔레토비 소녀』는 한국도서관협회 올해의 우수문학도서에 선정되었다.

강영숙은 2006년 대산창작기금 수혜자로 선정되었고, 2007년 일본 호세이대학교에서 객원연구원을 지냈다. 2008년 5월 한국문학번역원이 주최한 '서울, 젊은 작가들 축제'에 여러 작가들과 함께 참가했으며, 2009년 미국 아이오와대학교의 '국제창작프로그램'에 참가했다. 2013년에는 국제교류진흥회의 후원으로 소설가 김인숙, 브루스 풀턴 교수와 함께 미국 4개 대학에서 낭독회를 가졌으며, 2014년에 대산재단-UC버클리대학교의 체류작가 프로그램에 선정되었다. 1990년부터 현

tempts to settle down wherever she goes to no avail. Rina's journey, during which she crosses paths with all manner of unsavory characters, whose business dealings include murder, rape, human trafficking, drug distribution, and prostitution, is described in a uniquely dark comic tone where it becomes difficult to tell reality from illusion. In 2006 Kang received the 39th *Hankook Ilbo* Award for this novel. A translated excerpt of this novel was published in the December 2010 issue of *Azalea,* an annual Korean literature journal published by Harvard University. The novel was also published in Japanese by Gendaikikakushitsu in 2011, and is forthcoming in English in the latter half of 2014.

Her second novel *Writing Club* (2010) was a bildungsroman set in the backdrop of Bukchon (Gyedong), Seoul. It primarily presents a story of a mother and a daughter driven mad over the subject of writing. This novel received the 2011 Baek Shinae Literary Award and is currently being translated into English. Kang's third novel *Sad and Delightful Teletubby Girl*, which depicted the daily life of a runaway teenage girl, was selected as an example of particularly exemplary writing by the Ministry of

재까지 재단법인 대화문화아카데미에서 일하고 있으며 가족과 함께 서울에 살고 있다.

Culture, Sports, and Tourism and Arts Korea Council in 2013.

A recipient of the 2006 Daesan Young Writer's Creative Writing Fund, Kang was a visiting associate at Hosei University in Japan in 2007 and participated in the Seoul Young Writers' Festival sponsored by the Korea Literature Translation Institute in May 2008 and the University of Iowa International Writing Program in 2009. In 2013, Kang went on a reading tour throughout major universities in the U.S. with writer Kim In-suk and Prof. Bruce Fulton, with funding provided by the International Communication Foundation in Seoul. She was selected for the 2014 Daesan-Berkeley Writer-in-Residence Program and will stay in Berkeley, California, in 2014.

Kang has been working at the Korea Dialogue Academy (http://www.daemuna.or.kr) since 1990 and lives in Seoul with her family.

번역 **전승희** Translated by Jeon Seung-hee

전승희는 서울대학교와 하버드대학교에서 영문학과 비교문학으로 박사 학위를 받았으며, 현재 하버드대학교 한국학 연구소의 연구원으로 재직하며 아시아 문예 계간지 《ASIA》 편집위원으로 활동 중이다. 현대 한국문학 및 세계문학을 다룬 논문을 다수 발표했으며, 바흐친의 『장편소설과 민중언어』, 제인 오스틴의 『오만과 편견』 등을 공역했다. 1988년 한국여성연구소의 창립과 《여성과 사회》의 창간에 참여했고, 2002년부터 보스턴 지역 피학대 여성을 위한 단체인 '트랜지션하우스' 운영에 참여해 왔다. 2006년 하버드대학교 한국학 연구소에서 '한국 현대사와 기억'을 주제로 한 워크숍을 주관했다.

Jeon Seung-hee is a member of the Editorial Board of ***ASIA***, and a Fellow at the Korea Institute, Harvard University. She received a Ph.D. in English Literature from Seoul National University and a Ph.D. in Comparative Literature from Harvard University. She has presented and published numerous papers on modern Korean and world literature. She is also a co-translator of Mikhail Bakhtin's ***Novel and the People's Culture*** and Jane Austen's ***Pride and Prejudice***. She is a founding member of the Korean Women's Studies Institute and of the biannual Women's Studies' journal ***Women and Society*** (1988), and she has been working at 'Transition House,' the first and oldest shelter for battered women in New England. She organized a workshop entitled "The Politics of Memory in Modern Korea" at the Korea Institute, Harvard University, in 2006. She also served as an advising committee member for the Asia-Africa Literature Festival in 2007 and for the POSCO Asian Literature Forum in 2008.

감수 **데이비드 윌리엄 홍** Edited by David William Hong

데이비드 윌리엄 홍은 미국 일리노이주 시카고에서 태어났다. 일리노이대학교에서 영문학을, 뉴욕대학교에서 영어교육을 공부했다. 지난 2년간 서울에 거주하면서 처음으로 한국인과 아시아계 미국인 문학에 깊이 몰두할 기회를 가졌다. 현재 뉴욕에서 거주하며 강의와 저술 활동을 한다.

David William Hong was born in 1986 in Chicago, Illinois. He studied English Literature at the University of Illinois and English Education at New York University. For the past two years, he lived in Seoul, South Korea, where he was able to immerse himself in Korean and Asian-American literature for the first time. Currently, he lives in New York City, teaching and writing.

바이링궐 에디션 한국 대표 소설 067

트럭

2014년 4월 11일 초판 1쇄 인쇄 | 2014년 4월 18일 초판 1쇄 발행

지은이 강영숙 | **옮긴이** 전승희 | **펴낸이** 김재범
감수 데이비드 윌리엄 홍 | **기획** 정은경, 전성태, 이경재
편집 정수인, 이은혜 | **관리** 박신영 | **디자인** 이춘희
펴낸곳 (주)아시아 | **출판등록** 2006년 1월 27일 제406-2006-000004호
주소 서울특별시 동작구 서달로 161-1(흑석동 100-16)
전화 02.821.5055 | **팩스** 02.821.5057 | **홈페이지** www.bookasia.org
ISBN 979-11-5662-018-1 (set) | 979-11-5662-019-8 (04810)
값은 뒤표지에 있습니다.

Bi-lingual Edition Modern Korean Literature 067

Truck

Written by Kang Young-sook | **Translated by** Jeon Seung-hee
Published by Asia Publishers | 161-1, Seodal-ro, Dongjak-gu, Seoul, Korea
Homepage Address www.bookasia.org | **Tel**. (822).821.5055 | **Fax**. (822).821.5057
First published in Korea by Asia Publishers 2014
ISBN 979-11-5662-018-1 (set) | 979-11-5662-019-8 (04810)

〈바이링궐 에디션 한국 대표 소설〉 작품 목록(1~45)

도서출판 아시아는 지난 반세기 동안 한국에서 나온 가장 중요하고 첨예한 문제의식을 가진 작가들의 작품들을 선별하여 총 105권의 시리즈를 기획하였다. 하버드 한국학 연구원 및 세계 각국의 우수한 번역진들이 참여하여 외국인들이 읽어도 어색함이 느껴지지 않는 손색없는 번역으로 인정받았다. 이 시리즈는 세계인들에게 문학 한류의 지속적인 힘과 가능성을 입증하는 전집이 될 것이다.

바이링궐 에디션 한국 대표 소설 set 1

분단 Division

01 병신과 머저리-**이청준** The Wounded-**Yi Cheong-jun**
02 어둠의 혼-**김원일** Soul of Darkness-**Kim Won-il**
03 순이삼촌-**현기영** Sun-i Samch'on-**Hyun Ki-young**
04 엄마의 말뚝 1-**박완서** Mother's Stake I-**Park Wan-suh**
05 유형의 땅-**조정래** The Land of the Banished-**Jo Jung-rae**

산업화 Industrialization

06 무진기행-**김승옥** Record of a Journey to Mujin-**Kim Seung-ok**
07 삼포 가는 길-**황석영** The Road to Sampo-**Hwang Sok-yong**
08 아홉 켤레의 구두로 남은 사내-**윤흥길** The Man Who Was Left as Nine Pairs of Shoes-**Yun Heung-gil**
09 돌아온 우리의 친구-**신상웅** Our Friend's Homecoming-**Shin Sang-ung**
10 원미동 시인-**양귀자** The Poet of Wŏnmi-dong-**Yang Kwi-ja**

여성 Women

11 중국인 거리-**오정희** Chinatown-**Oh Jung-hee**
12 풍금이 있던 자리-**신경숙** The Place Where the Harmonium Was-**Shin Kyung-sook**
13 하나코는 없다-**최윤** The Last of Hanak'o-**Ch'oe Yun**
14 인간에 대한 예의-**공지영** Human Decency-**Gong Ji-young**
15 빈처-**은희경** Poor Man's Wife-**Eun Hee-kyung**

바이링궐 에디션 한국 대표 소설 set 2

자유 Liberty

16 필론의 돼지-**이문열** Pilon's Pig-**Yi Mun-yol**
17 슬로우 불릿-**이대환** Slow Bullet-**Lee Dae-hwan**
18 직선과 독가스-**임철우** Straight Lines and Poison Gas-**Lim Chul-woo**
19 깃발-**홍희담** The Flag-**Hong Hee-dam**
20 새벽 출정-**방현석** Off to Battle at Dawn-**Bang Hyeon-seok**

사랑과 연애 Love and Love Affairs

21 별을 사랑하는 마음으로-**윤후명** With the Love for the Stars-**Yun Hu-myong**
22 목련공원-**이승우** Magnolia Park-**Lee Seung-u**
23 칼에 찔린 자국-**김인숙** Stab-**Kim In-suk**
24 회복하는 인간-**한강** Convalescence-**Han Kang**
25 트렁크-**정이현** In the Trunk-**Jeong Yi-hyun**

남과 북 South and North

26 판문점-**이호철** Panmunjom-**Yi Ho-chol**
27 수난 이대-**하근찬** The Suffering of Two Generations-**Ha Geun-chan**
28 분지-**남정현** Land of Excrement-**Nam Jung-hyun**
29 봄 실상사-**정도상** Spring at Silsangsa Temple-**Jeong Do-sang**
30 은행나무 사랑-**김하기** Gingko Love-**Kim Ha-kee**

바이링궐 에디션 한국 대표 소설 set 3

서울 Seoul

31 눈사람 속의 검은 항아리-**김소진** The Dark Jar within the Snowman-**Kim So-jin**
32 오후, 가로지르다-**하성란** Traversing Afternoon-**Ha Seong-nan**
33 나는 봉천동에 산다-**조경란** I Live in Bongcheon-dong-**Jo Kyung-ran**
34 그렇습니까? 기린입니다-**박민규** Is That So? I'm A Giraffe-**Park Min-gyu**
35 성탄특선-**김애란** Christmas Specials-**Kim Ae-ran**

전통 Tradition

36 무자년의 가을 사흘-**서정인** Three Days of Autumn, 1948-**Su Jung-in**
37 유자소전-**이문구** A Brief Biography of Yuja-**Yi Mun-gu**
38 향기로운 우물 이야기-**박범신** The Fragrant Well-**Park Bum-shin**
39 월행-**송기원** A Journey under the Moonlight-**Song Ki-won**
40 협죽도 그늘 아래-**성석제** In the Shade of the Oleander-**Song Sok-ze**

아방가르드 Avant-garde

41 아겔다마-**박상륭** Akeldama-**Park Sang-ryoong**
42 내 영혼의 우물-**최인석** A Well in My Soul-**Choi In-seok**
43 당신에 대해서-**이인성** On You-**Yi In-seong**
44 회색 時-**배수아** Time In Gray-**Bae Su-ah**
45 브라운 부인-**정영문** Mrs. Brown-**Jung Young-moon**

바이링궐 에디션 한국 대표 소설 set 4

디아스포라 Diaspora

46 속옷-**김남일** Underwear-**Kim Nam-il**
47 상하이에 두고 온 사람들-**공선옥** People I Left in Shanghai-**Gong Sun-ok**
48 모두에게 복된 새해-**김연수** Happy New Year to Everyone-**Kim Yeon-su**
49 코끼리-**김재영** The Elephant-**Kim Jae-young**
50 먼지별-**이경** Dust Star-**Lee Kyung**

가족 Family

51 혜자의 눈꽃-**천승세** Hye-ja's Snow-Flowers-**Chun Seung-sei**
52 아베의 가족-**전상국** Ahbe's Family-**Jeon Sang-guk**
53 문 앞에서-**이동하** Outside the Door-**Lee Dong-ha**
54 그리고, 축제-**이혜경** And Then the Festival-**Lee Hye-kyung**
55 봄밤-**권여선** Spring Night-**Kwon Yeo-sun**

유머 Humor

56 오늘의 운세-**한창훈** Today's Fortune-**Han Chang-hoon**
57 새-**전성태** Bird-**Jeon Sung-tae**
58 밀수록 다시 가까워지는-**이기호** So Far, and Yet So Near-**Lee Ki-ho**
59 유리방패-**김중혁** The Glass Shield-**Kim Jung-hyuk**
60 전당포를 찾아서-**김종광** The Pawnshop Chase-**Kim Chong-kwang**